Julia's Magic

BOOKS BY ELEANOR CAMERON

The Mushroom Planet Books
The Wonderful Flight to the Mushroom Planet
Stowaway to the Mushroom Planet
Mr. Bass's Planetoid
A Mystery for Mr. Bass
Time and Mr. Bass

The Julia Books
Julia's Magic
That Julia Redfern
Julia and the Hand of God
A Room Made of Windows

Other Books for Young People
The Terrible Churnadryne
The Mysterious Christmas Shell
The Beast with the Magical Horn
A Spell Is Cast
The Court of the Stone Children
To the Green Mountains
Beyond Silence

Novel
The Unheard Music

Essays
The Green and Burning Tree: On the Writing
and Enjoyment of Children's Books

Julia's Magic

by Eleanor Cameron

illustrated by Gail Owens

E. P. DUTTON • NEW YORK

7552

Library of Congress Cataloging in Publication Data

Cameron, Eleanor, date
  Julia's magic.

  Summary: A broken perfume bottle and the threat
of losing their home cause a crisis in the Redfern
family that shakes Julia's belief in magic.
    1. Children's stories, American.
[1. Family life—Fiction]   I. Owens, Gail, ill.
II. Title.
PZ7.C143Jw   1984   [Fic]   84-8118
ISBN 0-525-44114-X

Published in the United States by E. P. Dutton,
2 Park Avenue, New York, N.Y. 10016

Published simultaneously in Canada by
Fitzhenry & Whiteside Limited, Toronto

Editor: Ann Durell   Designer: Julia Gran

Printed in the U.S.A.   W
10 9 8 7 6 5 4

and this one is for that
Holly Gregory

Contents

1

Discovery

Julia was making a bridge with twigs between two stones at the side of the creek in the park, when a football came sailing over her head. It landed not far from her, then bobbled along in its crazy, lop-ended, football way down into the canyon.

Kids were running everywhere, but not in the right direction. They didn't seem to have any idea at all where their football had gone, because bushes and trees stood between them and the canyon.

"But I know! I know!" Julia exclaimed in excitement. At once she ran across the grass and plunged down the steep bank beside the waterfall where the creek dropped into a leafy darkness. "Won't those kids be surprised when I bring them their ball. And they're big kids, too—and all boys. And *I'll* be the one to find it—*me,* Julia Redfern!"

She scrambled and slid through the thick bushes to the bottom of the bank. But that ball was nowhere to be seen. She made her way along the edge of the creek, slipping and getting her sandals as wet as if she'd been wading. The bottoms of her coveralls were sopping.

How quiet it was in here, except for the occasional call of a bird and the bubbling and gurgling and plunging of the creek, running down from the hills toward the bottom of the park. It pushed against boulders in a froth, then glided free into smooth, shallow, sunlit mirrors, only to boil against rocks again. Everything smelled so good after the April rains. There were new ferns everywhere.

Now suddenly Julia paused and stared. She leaned over and squinted into the shallow part, catching her breath in astonishment.

"Why, that's *gold* down there at the bottom—it *is,* it *is!* Thousands and millions and billions of bits of gold—" Yes, flakes of it were shining in the glancing sunlight, sliding and flowing, then settling into little pockets. She tried to scoop some of it up, but the pieces were too small and escaped her. "Oh, if I could just get enough of it," she whispered to herself, "if I could just find some really big pieces, then Mama and Daddy and Greg and me'd be *rich.* I bet anything there must be big pieces somewhere. Just to think of it, nobody else knowing about gold being here. Because if they did, they'd all be down gathering it up. There'd be hundreds and hundreds of people, all trying to get rich, like those trolls swarming into the dragon's cave. But there isn't anybody, not a soul. So they don't know." She chuckled with satisfaction.

There were scuffles up near the edge of the canyon, and she heard the kids beating around in the bushes, yelling at each other. She squatted down so they wouldn't see her and come lunging over the edge.

"Nobody must find out—nobody," she went on to herself. "And I'll never tell Maisie. Especially not Maisie Woollard, because she'd go right home and tell her father and mother, and Mrs. Woollard would go talking all over the neighborhood about it. But I'll bring Greg, and we'll have big spoons, and boxes to put the gold in. And we'll keep the secret until we have enough gold so Daddy can stay home from that adding-machine place he works in—"

That way, she thought as she scrabbled up the bank again, he could write his stories as long as he wanted to, all day, every day, and not just weekends and nights, when he was too tired. It was no way to write, he said, and no wonder he never got anything published. But he had to work because Mama didn't make enough at the music store to keep all four of them going. That's what Greg said.

Why, here was that old football, right in front of her, caught in the bare, sticking-out roots of a tree in the side of the canyon. She pulled it free and clutched it to her chest. It was hard getting up the bank with only one hand to hold by, and her sandals were squishy. But somehow she clawed her way up and, at the top, ran out into the open and over the bridge that crossed the creek below where the boys were searching.

"Got it!" she shouted. "I've *got* it!"

Someone caught sight of her and told the others. They made a rush for her, the whole mob of them, and the first to reach her grabbed the ball.

"What's the big idea!" he yelled at her in fury. "You little nut—running off with it—"

"Why, I didn't run off with it." Julia flared up in equal fury. "I *found* it—it was down in the canyon—" She couldn't believe that here she'd gotten their ball for them, and they were mad at her because they thought she'd stolen it.

They were all around her in a pack, those huge, hot, sweaty bodies—phew, did they *smell!* They shuffled her out of the way as if she were nothing but a thing, and were off across the bridge and the enormous lawn and had forgotten her in a second.

Why, there was Mama way off on the other side of the park, walking up and down calling "Julia—Ju-u-li-a! It's time to be go-ing—" But she was looking the wrong way. She'd been at old Mrs. Hatfield's across from the park, taking her some library books.

"Mama!" called Julia. "Here I am"—and before she was halfway over the grass—"Mama, guess what— guess what!" She ran and flung her arms around Mama's legs, then stood back and gazed up at her. "You'll never guess in a million years. First there was the—"

But Mama wasn't listening. "Julia Redfern, where in the name of heaven have you been? You're filthy, your feet and coveralls are soaking, and your face is scarlet. Playing in the brook! And you *didn't* go down in the canyon after I told you not to—?"

Had Mama said not to? Maybe—maybe—but Julia didn't remember. "Well, I'm trying to *tell* you— First there was the football. It came down right near me, and none of the kids knew where it went, but *I* knew, so I got it. And, Mama, listen—but don't you dare let on to anybody—promise me faithfully," and Julia grabbed Mama by the arms and spoke in a low, rasping whisper, "cross your heart and hope to die. Mama, I know where there's *gold.* There is! I saw it in the creek, but it was in such little pieces I couldn't get enough to show you. But it's there, and Greg and I can bring boxes and gather a whole lot so that Daddy—"

"Julia," and Mama was shaking her head and smiling, then took Julia by the hand and started away so briskly that Julia had to skip to keep up, "there's no gold in the creek. Do you think people wouldn't have taken it out long ago? That's just shiny sand—"

"Oh." Julia was bitterly disappointed. "I thought that—"

"What? I can't hear you." Mama leaned down.

"I thought that maybe, if Greg and I could get enough gold, we'd be rich, and then Daddy could stay home and write and write, and have something be printed the way he wants—"

Mama didn't answer for a moment. "Well, Julia," she said at last, "that was a fine thought, but I doubt very much if we'll ever be rich."

"But *why* not? *Why* couldn't we ever be? Aunt Alex and Uncle Hugh are—"

"Oh, Julia, you're too young to understand—"

"No, I'm not. Would Greg be?" demanded Julia jealously. "Too young?"

"Well, he's very grown-up in some ways for an eight-year-old, isn't he? But what I meant was, we'll never find any gold, and even if Daddy *did* get something published, something very important, a novel, it would take a long, long time for him even to start earning a living by writing. Oh, I don't know—" Mama sighed and was silent again while they hurried down the hill toward home. "But anyway," she said after a little, "look at what a day it is. And you're taking a picnic to the beach with Uncle Hugh."

Julia stopped in her tracks. How could she have forgotten? Well, she hadn't, really. She gave a leap and ran on down ahead. A picnic with Uncle Hugh at the beach! And it was a warm, sunny Saturday morning, with white clouds bowling across the sky and a little freshet of wind getting up every now and then.

Out there lay the bay, with the ferryboats moving across from Oakland to the docks of San Francisco, then coming back again. Even from here you could see their ghostly, curving wakes—the foam they shook out at the back of themselves as they made their way across the water. Soon she and Mama would be on one of those ferries, but not Greg, because he was out hiking up in the hills with his friend Bob. And not Daddy, because he was home at his typewriter. But here she was, in Berkeley, *now,* and after a while she'd be down there on the bay on one of those little specks of white. And the green, curving-over water would be making a hushing, rustling sound along the sides of the ferry and gulls would be flying right close overhead, swooping for their crusts the children always brought. It was so strange to think about, being up here at this moment, and then in a little bit, way off down there.

In about an hour and a half, all cleaned up, with her bathing suit on under her dress, she was leaning against the railing of the front deck of the ferry, watching those tiny buildings on the other side of the bay coming closer and closer. On one of the hills of San Francisco stood Aunt Alex and Uncle Hugh's house. And large, beautiful Aunt Alex and Mama would start off in Aunt Alex's large, handsome car and have lunch someplace elegant. Then Mama would buy socks and underwear on sale at Capwell's. And Aunt Alex would probably buy perfume and gloves, or maybe another pink nightgown with lace all over.

And Julia and Uncle Hugh would be plunging around in the ocean, or at least Uncle Hugh would. Julia didn't exactly plunge.

2

A Most Horrible
Surprise

But first of all, before she could get into Uncle
Hugh's red runabout with the top down and start off
for the beach, Julia had to go to the bathroom, she was
so excited.

Aunt Alex's new cook and housekeeper, Hulda,
brought out the picnic basket, "ab-solutely *stuffed* with
food," said Aunt Alex. She and Mama were standing
on the porch of the big house, watching, while Hulda
went out to the car and talked to Uncle Hugh about
the best place to put the basket among the other things
he had in the back. Aunt Alex was talking about Hulda
in a low voice. She'd been with them for just three
months now and was proving to be quiet, quick and,
Aunt Alex would continue to hope, dependable and

honest. And, of course, she was a marvelous cook, as Julia and Greg and Mama and Daddy already knew. Her chief virtue, said Aunt Alex.

Now Uncle Hugh was busy peering under the hood of the car to see that everything was just as it should be, then decided he must go in and wash his hands. Julia, hopping up and down with impatience, decided she'd better go, too. Or rather Mama decided. "No use putting it off, Julia, the way you usually do."

In she went and heard Uncle Hugh running water in the downstairs bathroom, so she nipped upstairs to go to the other one, but paused at Aunt Alex's bedroom door.

And that was the fatal moment.

How good this room always smelled, like all Aunt Alex's belongings, her clothes, her handkerchiefs, the pillows she leaned against. It was so beautiful in here, it was like a queen's bedroom. Never any mess, like in Julia's and Greg's little rooms, or even in Mama and Daddy's, because Daddy had his desk in there, where he did his writing, and that desk was never anything but a mess and nothing must ever be touched.

In the evening, Aunt Alex might go up to bed early with one of her sick headaches, so she could read mysteries in comfort (and eat chocolates, Julia happened to know). And when it was time for the Redferns to leave on the late ferry, Julia and Greg would be sent upstairs to say goodbye. That is, if there was still a line of light showing under Aunt Alex's door. They'd knock and go in and stand in line at the side of the bed, just like for a queen, to lean over Aunt Alex's plump face and kiss her good-night. Aunt Alex would always hold Greg by the hand to talk to him about school and whatever fun he was having, which left Julia to sit on the edge of the bed and yawn and yawn until her jaws cracked. But Aunt Alex never wanted Greg to go, no matter how much *he* wanted to.

Now Julia stole inside and gazed around, especially at all those shining little bottles on Aunt Alex's glass-topped dressing table with a large mirror at the back. She went over and sank onto the cushioned seat, reached out a hand and picked up her favorite bottle, the one with the golden scrolls all over it, very delicate and fine. The stopper, cut into the shape of a round little animal with golden eyes, glowed in the sunlight slanting in from the long windows. Julia had always loved that little animal. It was a fairy creature, she'd decided—magical, which was why it shone so in rainbow colors. Carefully she pulled it out to take a sniff, when—the most horrible surprise!

The stopper slid right out of her hand as if it had a small, wicked life of its own, fell onto the glass top of the dressing table, and parted neatly into two halves, right through the little animal's body.

Julia was so stunned she dropped the bottle. She stopped breathing for five whole seconds, then went

burning hot all over, the blood tingling and pricking in her veins. She picked up the bottle and stood it upright, picked up the two halves of the stopper, pressed them together, and slid the bottom part back into the neck.

Why, you'd never know the top was split apart! It was like magic—the little animal's magic. She need never tell a single soul. The relief—the relief, and that the bottle itself hadn't broken. He was as good as new, that little crouched-up shape with the golden eyes. Were they watching her? She reached out and put the bottle at the back of the dressing table behind the others and tiptoed lightly, ever so lightly, out of the room.

She listened. Aunt Alex and Mama and Hulda were laughing out on the front porch. And Uncle Hugh— where was he? She crept downstairs and heard him whistling in his study across from the bathroom in the side hall, then a drawer closed in his desk. Quickly, quickly, without thinking why, she ran towards the front door. But she *must* go to the bathroom, so she turned back—and met Uncle Hugh coming around the corner into the main hall.

"Skip along, now, Julia—be quick," he said. "We're all ready to go—" He gave her a pat on the head as he passed.

She rushed to the bathroom, tore off a yard of paper, and barely remembered to flush the toilet. When she came out, Mama and Aunt Alex were standing at the foot of the stairs.

"There you are, Julia—" cried Aunt Alex.

"And remember," said Mama, "you're to be back here by four o'clock at the latest. We have our ferry to catch—"

"Goodbye, goodbye!" everybody called after them when Uncle Hugh and Julia got in the red runabout and whizzed away. Everything, she thought, was as perfect as it could possibly be.

She ran across the sand under the vast bowl of the sky with the whole ocean spread in front of her and seeming to rise, oddly enough, slightly uphill. The openness of sea and sky and sand always filled her with such joy she couldn't speak. Uncle Hugh spread out the blanket and put the picnic basket on it, then slipped off his sweater and shirt and trousers, and there he was in his navy blue and white striped bathing suit. "It's almost one o'clock, Julia, so do you want to eat now, then wait awhile, or shall we go in and have a swim first?"

Julia, hopping like a sand flea, had whipped her dress and slip over her head and yanked off her shoes and socks, and they were all ready to go in—Julia in her bright new red suit.

"Swim first—swim first—" she shouted, and was off over the sand down to the gleaming stretch of hard, wet part where the little sandpipers were hunting in coveys, for *what* Julia could never figure out—some tiny sea bug—pecking and pecking and pecking, quick, quick, then running off ahead of her on twinkling, almost invisible sticks of legs, as if they went on wheels. *"Peep, peep, peep, peep!"* they cried, warning each other. They were so funny, those little furiously busy bodies, she always had to laugh to see them whisk away.

She danced in the surf—oh, it was *cold.* But Uncle Hugh paid not the slightest attention to the cold, just splashed past her and was swimming out in a second. Then he ploughed back in and caught her up and took her out to swing her over the waves. And she wasn't a bit scared, only almost more worked up than she could bear.

Then he tossed her down on the sand and she promised faithfully, as she always did, that she wouldn't budge from their bit of territory in front of the blanket, just play right where he could keep an eye on her as he swam out and looked back every now and then. And the lady on her blanket a little way off from theirs winked at Uncle Hugh and nodded, meaning, Julia knew, that she'd keep an eye out. So then Uncle Hugh went back in, knowing that she would not wander off, because if she did, he would never bring her again. *Never.*

He swam and swam until she could barely see him,

but she was used to this. He'd done it before, then he'd
turn and swim along the coast, first to the right, then
back the other way, as if he couldn't swim enough.
He'd been a champion swimmer before he married
Aunt Alex, and he had silver cups lined up on the
bookcase in his bedroom.

"But why *before,* Uncle Hugh?" Julia had asked.
"Why not *now?*" Oh, because he didn't have the time,
he said. He had other things to do.

"Well, why don't you be a champion weekends,
then?" she'd persisted.

"Julia, Julia," Aunt Alex had laughed, when Julia
said this in front of her, "I have other things for Uncle
Hugh to do weekends than be a champion swimmer,
for heaven's sake."

"Well, *what* things?" demanded Julia. What could
possibly be more important than being a champion
swimmer!

"Oh, places to go, people to visit," said Aunt Alex.

Oh, bore, bore, bore, thought Julia resentfully.
Poor Uncle Hugh. Now he was coming back in. But
Julia noticed that people were beginning to gather in
a little crowd, and everybody was pointing out beyond
the breakers. Why? There was Uncle Hugh—she
could see his arms going up and down. He was doing
the crawl, the way he always did, and could he swim
fast. But they weren't pointing at him, but to something farther out.

Now here he was, walking out of the surf, pinching his nose to get the water out of it, and shaking his head to get the water out of his ears. Then he noticed the people pointing and went over to them, with Julia running along behind, and the lady, too, who'd been keeping an eye on her.

"Look!" they said. "Someone out there—an old man—there's his white head—he's been signaling—"

"Come on," said Uncle Hugh abruptly, and grabbed a young fellow with shiny black curly hair and tanned skin and big muscles and the whitest teeth Julia had ever seen. "Come on, let's go and get him."

But the young fellow wouldn't. He couldn't swim a stroke, he said. Everybody was astonished, he was so big and handsome and tan. So Uncle Hugh went back in, and soon he was way out and then pulling slowly toward shore with the white-haired man at his side. Now he was dragging him out of the water and then laid him on the sand face down with one arm under his head. Next, to Julia's surprise, Uncle Hugh straddled the old man's behind, kneeling over him with a leg on each side, and began pushing at his back, up toward his head, hard, then let go, pushed upward again, let go, pushed and let go, and kept this up for the longest time. Water was coming out of the old man's mouth, but he didn't move. His eyes were closed and he was all loose looking. His nose seemed like a bone, it was so white.

"He's gone," said the lady, who had an arm across Julia's shoulders as if they were friends. "He's gone—it's no use," she said in a low voice, shaking her head. "Too late—it's no *use*. But where are his people? Was he alone?" Nobody seemed to know.

But what did she mean! That the man was *dead?* *Drowned?* Julia felt a coldness all the way to her insides. She knew very well what "dead" was. She'd seen the finch Patchy had brought in, its smooth, coppery-red breast feathers in ugly disarray, its claws drawn up, its bright eyes glazed over, and then the small rabbit, limp and still, its ears fallen. She'd hated Patchy violently for a whole day after each killing, though she couldn't keep it up. But she'd never seen a dead man before, and here he was, lying right at her feet and his face was gray. Everybody was terribly silent, just watching.

Then, slowly, the man began to stir, moving his arms a little, his hands, then his legs. "Ohhhhh!" sighed everybody, just as if they were one person sending up one thankful sigh. But Julia began crying, though she didn't know why. The lady leaned down and drew her close. "Never mind," she said. "He's been saved and everything's all right—"

"My uncle saved him!" shouted Julia. "That's my Uncle Hugh and he's saved him—he's a champion swimmer, and he has all sorts of cups on his bookcase. You should just see them. Great big silver—"

But nobody was listening. Uncle Hugh and several of the others were getting the old man to his feet and everyone yelled "Hoo-raaay!" and then moved in so close that Julia was pushed aside and couldn't see a thing that was happening. Now everybody began going back up the beach and someone said that they were taking the old fellow to the bathhouse so that he could be driven off in an ambulance. After a little Julia saw Uncle Hugh coming down to the beach again.

"Uncle Hugh—is he still alive?"

"Still alive, Julia." She and the lady had gone back to the blanket and picnic basket. "Still alive and perfectly fine. But they want him to be checked over, just to be sure. He said this was his first swim of the year, and he went out a bit too far and knew he couldn't make it back. He was almost gone, because the waves kept slapping him down every time he came up, and he couldn't get his breath." Uncle Hugh was quiet for a second or two. "That was a narrow squeak," he said.

"What's 'a narrow squeak'?"

"A close call. If they hadn't seen him, and I hadn't got there when I did, just in the *nick* of time, he'd have been a goner."

"A narrow squeak." Julia liked that; that was good. Like when a mouse flashes into its hole right in front of the cat's paw. Squeak, squeak! Cat's out of luck— same as the sea. Didn't get the old man after all.

"And now," said Uncle Hugh, "would you open the basket, Julia, and lay everything out, so we can commence our feast? And would you join us?" he said to the lady, giving her a little quick smile. "I know we have far more than enough. And I thank you for keeping an eye on this young person."

But the lady said reluctantly, looking at Uncle Hugh in a certain way, that she couldn't join them, worse luck, because she had to go. She had an appointment. She was sorry, very sorry, and by the way she smiled at Uncle Hugh, Julia thought she really was—*extreme*ly sorry. Off she went, waving goodbye, gathered up her towel and beach bag, and waved again.

Julia began unpacking all the delicious things Hulda had put in the basket. She felt like Mole when he and Ratty went on their picnic by the river and Mole could hardly believe people really did this sort of blissful thing, because he himself had led such a dull sort of life by comparison. Daddy was reading *The Wind in the Willows* to her and Greg every evening for half an hour after Julia went to bed, a book that told all about Mole and Toad and Ratty.

All at once, just as she was taking out packages that she was sure, by their shape and darkness, must be slices of chocolate cake, she sat back on her heels and studied Uncle Hugh. "She thinks you're handsome."

Uncle Hugh of course knew who Julia meant. "Fiddle-faddle," he said. "Now choose. Start in. Because if you don't, I'm going to eat everything up *at once!*"

3

---◆---

Young Man-About-Town

"Uncle Hugh—" Julia took a bite out of her ham sandwich and chewed for a moment, thinking. "Did you have lots of lady friends before you married Aunt Alex?"

"Lots of lady friends!" exclaimed Uncle Hugh, his eyebrows going up. "I should say I did. Nothing serious—well, mostly nothing serious. But lots of them."

"And did you have fun?"

"Oh, I enjoyed myself—I was a great enjoyer in those days, even at work. But then I didn't have the responsibilities at the bank that I do now."

"What's that, responsi— what you said?"

"Well, duties and jobs you have to be sure will turn out right—that people expect you to see to, knowing they can trust you. Oh, in those days, I seemed to have all the time in the world. Nights, there'd be parties, and weekends I'd be invited up to the mountains to stay with friends in their cottages, and out to the country and to the beach. I suppose I was what you'd call a young man-about-town."

"What's that mean?"

"A young man invited everywhere, having the time of his life. The absolute time of his life! Just think, that was only twelve or thirteen years ago—" Uncle Hugh looked off across the ocean, holding his sandwich unbitten, and Julia saw he was smiling to himself, just slightly. What was he remembering? "Say, I know," he said. "On the way home I could show you where I lived then, where my apartment was, in a big gray rambling house in a garden, an apartment hotel, with a large airy dining room where we all ate, and a smaller private dining room where we could give parties. And I had a corner room up on the third floor that looked out over the entire city. You know, I'd like to see it again, Julia. I'd like to drive past and see how it looks now. How about that? On the way home."

Mama was standing out on the front porch at Aunt Alex's when Julia and Uncle Hugh got back. And she came down the steps in a hurry with all her packages when she saw them, just as if she didn't want to waste a minute. Aunt Alex was standing in the doorway.

"Hugh!" said Mama. "It's almost four thirty and you promised to be back by four. Where on earth have you been?"

"Sorry, Celia—we had a little journey to make into the past, Julia and I—but don't you worry. Hop in, we'll be down in good time. Have I ever failed you?"

"No, you haven't, Hugh, that I'll have to admit," said Mama, getting in beside Julia. "But you're a bad one all the same, and Julia, too."

"Goodbye, Aunt Alex," shouted Julia excitedly. "No time to hear about everything. Uncle Hugh *saved* a man—!"

All the way downtown Julia told Mama how Uncle Hugh had saved the poor man from drowning, and how he couldn't get the big, handsome, tanned one with the white teeth and muscles to go in with him because he couldn't swim a stroke, and how they all thought the old man was dead but Uncle Hugh pushed on his back and pushed and pushed and got him alive again. Uncle Hugh didn't say a word, he was so busy zipping his way through the traffic to get to the ferry building on time. And they made it, Mama and Julia hurrying up the gangplank just as the man with the rope was going to unwind it from the big iron thing on the dock to let the ferry go free. And all the pilings on either side groaned and squeaked, being forced backward as the ferry drew out, and there they were, Mama and Julia, safe on board. Daddy would have his dinner on time after all, and not around eight o'clock as he would have if they'd had to take the later one.

They sat peacefully together out on the rear deck, watching the gulls and the view across the water back to San Francisco, where Uncle Hugh, said Mama, would be almost home by now, and then he'd go in, thought Julia, and tell Aunt Alex all about saving the man from drowning. Would she be proud of him? Or would she just smile her little smile you could never quite understand? Julia had noticed that Uncle Hugh hadn't said anything about going up to see his apartment, or about Larkie—Mrs. Larkin, who used to be his landlady—so Julia thought she wouldn't either.

"—and did you have a happy time, Julia? Apart from Uncle Hugh having to save the man from being drowned?" Mama was asking.

"Mama, were you surprised when Uncle Hugh married Aunt Alex?"

"Good heavens, what a question!"

"Well, I just wondered—"

"Yes, I think I was. None of us knew Aunt Alex."

"And did you like Nikki, the one he thought he was going to marry?"

"Now, what's all this? What have you and Uncle Hugh been talking about?"

"But *did* you, Mama?"

"Well, yes, I did. Very much, indeed. In fact, I— well, but, anyway—that's Uncle Hugh's business. I'm surprised he told you."

"In fact you *what,* Mama?" How Julia hated it when

grown-ups started to say things, and then stopped at the most interesting part because you were only a child.

"I *said,* Julia, that *that's* Uncle Hugh's business," Mama repeated in her finishing-off tone that Julia knew very well from experience.

"*Do* I look just like Uncle Hugh?" Julia was remembering what Larkie had said, thinking that Julia was Uncle Hugh's daughter.

"What a question-box you are! Yes, you do look a good deal like him—or like me. It's the family look."

"And Greg looks more like Daddy. Mama, don't the gentlemen usually propose to the ladies, and not the ladies to the gentlemen?"

Mama closed her eyes and shook her head and then gave a little laugh. She looked down at Julia and her eyes were merry. "Just what are you getting at now, Julia Redfern? Yes, the gentleman usually *does* do the proposing. In fact, I would say he always does."

"But, *why? Why* can't the lady ask?"

"Because—well, because it wouldn't be ladylike."

"Then Aunt Alex wasn't ladylike, was she?"

Mama studied Julia for a second. "So that's it," she said. "Uncle Hugh told you. But I suppose it's all right. They've told their friends and laugh about it, at least Aunt Alex does. She doesn't seem to mind people knowing. Yes, I hear she *did* do the proposing and thinks it's very amusing."

"Uncle Hugh was shy, wasn't he?"

"Well, he was never shy with anyone else to my knowing," said Mama sharply.

"But Aunt Alex always got what she wanted, didn't she?" persisted Julia, filled with sudden resentment. "Even though Uncle Hugh *was* going to marry Nikki."

"Now that will do, Julia. We will not say another word about it."

And they didn't. Because Julia knew it would be no use trying to. For some reason. And she sat there remembering Uncle Hugh's room at the hotel, very big, with a fireplace, and how they'd stood in front of the window just in *the very spot* where Aunt Alex had proposed to him. And then she saw the garden at Nikki's house in the pale light of dusk with Uncle Hugh and Nikki walking up and down, up and down, and Uncle Hugh trying to tell her that he was going to marry Aunt Alex, and when he did, Nikki looking up at him and saying that about Aunt Alex always getting her own way sooner or later about everything and then turning and going into the house and shutting the door. And that was all, and he'd never seen her again. What a sad story, like a fairy tale. And maybe Nikki was married now and had children and didn't care a bit about Uncle Hugh anymore. Not a single bit.

"Julia, for goodness sake, stop scratching!" exclaimed Mama suddenly. "What on earth is the matter with you? First one leg and then the other, and now your arms. Let me see— Why, child, you're covered, simply covered. Poison oak!" And Mama stared down at Julia with accusing eyes. "*So*—you went into the canyon after all. And I told you not to. I said you could play on the bridge. You could play by the brook. But you were *not* to go into the canyon. And you did. And now look at you."

Julia leaned over to examine her legs. And there were those terrible little white bumps, strings of them, up and down her legs and there on her arms, too. And where she'd given an especially hard dig, some bloody places.

She sat back with a heavy, fateful feeling. Just as Mama said, she was covered. It would be awful while it lasted, she knew, because she'd had poison oak before.

Worse luck, when she and Mama were walking up the street from Shattuck Avenue, where they'd gotten off the train that had brought them from the Oakland docks, there was Maisie coming out of the grocery store on the corner. She went along with them all the way home and bounced over to Julia when Julia got on the other side of Mama so Maisie wouldn't see the poison oak. But it was no use. That sharp-eyed Maisie Woollard noticed right off.

"Oh, Mrs. Redfern, look at Julia's *face*—and her

neck! Mama, Mama," she yelped, now that they were near home, and there was Mrs. Woollard out in front of her house, watering. "*Mama,* you should just see Julia—*poison oak!*"

Mrs. Woollard hung her hose carefully over the fence so that it sprayed across the grass, and came and peered at Julia. And Julia's mouth pulled itself down at both corners and she glared up at Mrs. Woollard.

"Tchk!" said Mrs. Woollard. "That child! There's only one place around here with poison oak in it that I know of, and that's the canyon up at the park. But I've forbidden Maisie ever to go there, and of course she never does. You know, my mother was clearing poison oak off a hillside and she just hauled it up and threw it in big piles, but never got it. She'd never had poison oak and never would, so *she* thought. But wherever the roots, with the juice of them, touched her arms, there came to be big black holes, the most terrible things you ever saw in your life. And they were months going away, and she had great scars afterwards. Had 'em for the rest of her life, she did—"

"Oooh, *Jul*ia!" cried Maisie delightedly, hopping like a jack-in-the-box, "did you pull up any roots?"

Julia gave her a furious shove. "Don't be dumb, how *could* I?"

"And I heard of another woman," went on Mrs. Woollard, though Mama was edging away because she wanted to get on across the street and start dinner,

"who built a big bonfire of poison oak, and the wind got up and blew the smoke right into her eyes and she went blind—stark, staring blind—just from the—"

"Oh, Mrs. *Wool*lard!" exclaimed Mama in exasperation. "I simply must go now—we're late as it is." And she caught Julia by the hand and hurried her over to their own house so fast it was as if she were escaping.

"Mama," said Julia breathlessly, "do you suppose *I'll*—?"

"No, of course you won't, Julia. *Really*— Some people—" and there was Patchy, come out to greet them, tail high, his mouth opening in little, quick, questioning, almost soundless greetings, "Mya-ah-ah-ah?"

"Oh, Patchy," said Julia, catching him up, "I've got poison oak again." But the minute she put her face into his fragrant, silky fur, she felt better. At least she wasn't going to go blind, because there hadn't been any bonfire. And there'd be no big black holes in her arms because she hadn't pulled up any roots.

When she got inside, she heard Mama say in a low voice to Daddy as he came out of their bedroom, "And I told her she could play on the bridge, or by the creek, but that she must *not* go into the canyon—and now, here she is, simply covered—"

Daddy came and looked gravely down at Julia. "Poor old Julia," he said. "Your sins have been revealed." He swept her up and gave her a big hug and a kiss. "Poor kid—"

Greg had heard everything, as usual.

"You can go into the first room," he said, "and you can go into the second room, but you must *not* go into the little room at the end of the hall."

Julia knew exactly what he meant. Bluebeard, saying that to Lady Ann when he gave her his keys. But as soon as Bluebeard went away, Lady Ann *did* go into the little room at the end of the hall and found all the bones of the women who'd been his wives before her, because they, like her, had disobeyed and gone into that little room.

"I forgot," she said.

"You mean you just didn't want to remember," said Greg.

"I *hate* you."

She didn't want any dinner, but Mama thought that that was mostly because she'd had such a huge picnic, and brought calamine lotion and painted it all over Julia's legs and arms, and her neck and her face, wherever the bumps had come up in rows. All she wanted was bread and milk, the hot milk poured over buttered bread cut into pieces, with raisins and a little sugar sprinkled on top. And Patchy-cat came and got up beside her and curled close into the curve of her leg on top of the sheet. That was all Julia wanted over her—just the sheet.

And while Mama and Daddy and Greg talked in companionable tones in the kitchen over their dinner, laughing about something every once in a while, Julia told Sister, whom nobody could see but Julia, all about the day at the beach.

After dinner, Daddy came in with *The Wind in the Willows* to see if she was still awake, and Greg came along too, to listen to another chapter of the story.

"Daddy, would you read the part about the picnic over again?"

"But we've *had* that," said Greg impatiently. "Let's go on—"

"Oh, just the little bit where Mole unpacks the picnic basket?" begged Julia.

So Daddy settled himself in Julia's only chair, and Greg hunched up at the bottom of her bed, leaning against the wall, and Daddy turned back near the beginning. Sister listened, too, and Patchy-cat, opening a green eye now and then.

" 'What's inside it?' asked the Mole, wriggling with curiosity.

" 'There's cold chicken inside it,' replied the Rat briefly, 'coldtonguecoldhamcoldbeefpickledgherkins-saladfrenchrollscresssandwichespottedmeatginger-beerlemonadesodawater—'

" 'O stop, stop,' cried the Mole in ecstasies: 'This is too much!'

" 'Do you really think so?' inquired the Rat seriously. 'It's only what I always take on these little excursions; and the other animals are always telling me that I'm a mean beast and cut it *very* fine!' "

"Just think," said Julia, "it's exactly what we had— ham and pickles and lemonade. *And* chocolate cake, besides. Oh, I do love Hulda!"

4

In a Strange Country

Julia went to sleep thinking about Hulda and how lucky Aunt Alex was to have her to cook for them and keep house. And all at once . . .

There they were, she and Hulda, on a train, but such a train as Julia had never been in before. They were in a little room, and there was a corridor running along the side of the train just outside their door. Through the glass of the door you could see the passengers going past along the corridor, which was like a very narrow hall. And one by one, men and women came into their little room and put their luggage up onto the racks overhead. Then they sat down and pretended not to look at each other, but did, out of the sides of their eyes. And Julia looked at them, each one, very thoroughly, until Hulda leaned over and whispered to her not to stare.

"Where are we, Hulda?"

"In England," said Hulda comfortably, just as if it were the usual thing for Hulda and Julia to be in England.

Oh! So here they were where Uncle Hugh and Mama had been born, across the sea. And this was the kind of train, with little rooms for the passengers, that Uncle Hugh and Mama had always told her about. She gave a wriggle of excitement.

"Are we going to visit somebody?" But Hulda gave her a mysterious sidelong glance as if it were a secret. Then a twinkle came into her eyes, and she seemed to give in and decide to let Julia know.

"We're going to visit your English family," she said, as if it had been a surprise she'd been saving up, "your mama and all the boys—"

"Who are all the boys?"

"Why, your uncles!" exclaimed Hulda. "Your uncles, Julia—Uncle Hugh and Uncle Artie and Uncle Will and Uncle Dick—"

Julia gave another wriggle of excitement, and then happened to look down and saw that Hulda must have bumped her leg. It was all bandaged up, and this made Julia's stomach feel funny.

"Why, Hulda, what did you do?"

"Oh, something happened at your Aunt Alex's, and

I hurt myself," was all Hulda would say. She didn't seem to want to talk about it, and her tone was so stern that Julia knew she wasn't to go on. But she wasn't afraid of Hulda. She loved her.

Now the other people in the little room began taking down their suitcases and unpacking their picnic lunches out of them: cheese sandwiches and ham sandwiches and chicken sandwiches, and pickles and apples and oranges and chocolate cake and bottles of lemonade. It smelled so good, all that food. But Julia and Hulda didn't seem to have any suitcases.

"Don't we have any lunch, Hulda?"

"No," said Hulda, "but don't you worry. We'll get off at the next stop and buy something, then get right back on again."

"Well, *I'll* get off, Hulda. It would be too hard for you with your hurt leg. I'll take care of you."

"No, no," said Hulda, shaking her head. "I'd never let you get off by yourself. We'll both get out, and I'll stay right by the train and watch while you go over to the station buffet and get us something."

When the train finally drew in to the next stop, they got up. And Julia was so hungry by that time she could hardly endure it, watching everybody else eat, and smelling the ham and oranges and cake. But Hulda had to go very slowly along the narrow corridor because of her leg hurting her, and Julia was frantic the train would start up again. But the conductor told them they had ten minutes yet, so *that* was all right.

They both got down onto the station platform and Hulda gave Julia some money and told her what to buy and Julia ran over and tried to ask for rolls with meat inside and two oranges. But there was such a crowd of people nobody would pay any attention to her, and they shoved her carelessly aside as if she didn't matter at all.

Now Hulda was calling to her, desperately, to come back—come back. It didn't matter about the food, so Julia ran to her and Hulda told her to get up in the doorway, quick, and to lean down and stretch out her hand so that Hulda would have something to hold on to. Julia hopped up and turned and was just about to stretch her hand down to Hulda when the train began to move. Someone snatched her inside, the door snapped closed—and Hulda was gone, left on the platform, and Julia was screaming at the top of her lungs, "Hulda—Hulda—! Stop, oh, please stop! Oh, Hulda —she's left behind—"

And Julia was awake, with her throat aching and her heart pounding most painfully.

"Oh, Hulda," she whispered, "*Hulda!* I would never leave you—I'd never, *never* let the train go away and leave you—"

But even though she knew that it had been a dream, still she felt the grief and terror she'd felt on the train. She'd *told* Hulda she'd take care of her. But what could she have done? Lying there in the dark, she tried and tried to get Hulda back on the train before the door snapped closed. But it was no use, she never could. That dream was too strong for her.

All the next day Julia was in a fever, with her poison oak driving her mad and Mama telling her to try not to scratch because the yellow stuff was beginning to come out of the little bumps. Every time she scratched, Mama said, if she got it on her hands and touched another part of herself, she would only spread it. So finally Mama put gauze bandages on her wherever the poison oak was worst, which made her hotter than ever. And when she cried and the tears ran down, she somehow got the idea that the poison oak would travel up through the tears to her eyes.

"Oh, Julia," said Mama, "of course it won't."

"But don't touch your eyes," said Daddy. "Here, I'll read to you," and he read her three stories out of her book of Japanese fairy tales. After he had kissed her good-night and turned out the light, and left the door open just an inch or two so she could hear what was going on, she remembered the little room on the train. She would have to tell Uncle Hugh her dream and ask him if Hulda was all right—if she was home again, safe.

5

What Can the Matter Be?

The house was quiet. She got up to go to the bathroom, but couldn't seem to find her way to the door into the hall. And when she opened the door, it was the wrong one—she was all turned around. There was a faint light from the streetlamp and she knew, because of the cool, fragrant air flowing in, that she was going into the garden. She had opened one of the French doors that led outside instead of the one into the hall.

"Patchy?" she called. But there was no Patchy. He'd gone a-hunting.

Now she could make out the vague outlines of the trees, but things were getting very small, and then very large—they weren't themselves at all. She closed the door and found her way across the room, out of the other door and into the bathroom. And she could hear

Mama in the kitchen talking to someone. But no one answered her, so she must be talking on the phone.

"But I can't believe it, dear. I just can't—it's so unfair." Silence. "But surely it won't be for good, will it?" Silence. "Oh, I see— Why, that's dreadful, but you mustn't let it go on. Can I do anything?" Silence. "Oh, but that won't help. It'll only make things worse." Silence. "But that's not like you. I've never known you like this before." Silence. "Well, of course, whenever you want to. You know you can, anytime. But what about Alex? Do you suppose she'll just continue to—?" Silence. "Oh, well, I suppose so—it just seems so—well, I don't know. Nothing like this has ever happened before, and I don't know how to take it." Silence. "All right, then, Hugh—we'll see you tomorrow evening."

After she came out of the bathroom, Julia stood in the hall, trying to get straight what Mama had been talking about to Uncle Hugh, but she couldn't. Her head felt like an old pillow; she wasn't even sure she could make it out to the kitchen through the dark living room.

"Mama?" She stumbled around to the kitchen door, and there was Mama sitting at the breakfast table with the lamp on, staring away at nothing. She looked up at Julia and held out her hand. Julia went to her and for a little, Mama didn't say anything, but sat there smoothing Julia's wildly rumpled hair.

"Uncle Hugh," she said at last. "He was just ask-

ing if he could come over tomorrow after work."

"For dinner, do you mean?"

"Yes, for dinner—"

"But what about Aunt Alex?" When had Uncle Hugh ever come to dinner without her?

"Oh, Aunt Alex," said Mama in a peculiar tone. "*She's* gone to visit some friends, and Uncle Hugh doesn't like being alone in that big house—doing everything for himself."

"But Hulda's there." Or *was* she there? She'd been on a train.

Mama didn't say anything, only got up and took Julia back to her room.

Well, Julia just couldn't figure out what was going on. *Some*thing puzzling!

The next day, Monday, Gramma came over to take care of her while everybody was gone, Mama and Daddy at work, and Greg at school. First off, Gramma changed Julia's bandages and that hurt, because they stuck. But she did it gently, remembering the other time Julia had had poison oak.

"Julia, Julia," she said, "after your mother telling you *not* to go into the canyon! Well, you'll know better next time, I'll wager. Surely by now you've learned your lesson. But I never did know such a young one for getting into scrapes of her own making."

"It wasn't my own making the time I backed into the

steam when Greg took the kettle off the stove and I got a burned sausage on my arm," exclaimed Julia indignantly.

By "a burned sausage" she meant that the steam from the kettle had made a burn on the back of her arm in the shape of a sausage. Oh, how that had hurt! And Mama had soaked it and soaked it in ice-cold water out of the icebox and the burn went away in no time. That's what the pioneers did, she said, when they didn't have anything else to put on, and it was the best thing you could do.

But Julia wasn't thinking about the burn anymore. She was thinking about Mama on the phone last night. "Gramma, what's the matter with Aunt Alex and Uncle Hugh?"

Gramma shot her a sharp, startled glance. "What do you mean, what's the matter? They're perfectly well, so far as I know."

"But I didn't mean exactly *that*—"

"Well, I'm sure I don't know what you *do* mean. And now I've got to get this house straightened up and go and do the shopping."

That night, just before dinner, Julia heard Greg and Daddy at the front door, and then Uncle Hugh's voice. Julia shouted and leaped out of bed and went racing into the front room. And Uncle Hugh held out his arms and was about to toss her up the way he always did, when he stopped and stood there, staring at her.

"Great *Scott,* Julia—what's *hap*pened to you?"

For a second or two, Julia felt proud to be the object of such a display of astonishment. But then Greg, always ready to be helpful, took it on himself to tell Uncle Hugh just what a dunce Julia had been not to recognize poison oak when she saw it.

"Well, poor old Julia," said Uncle Hugh, and he was about to pick her up anyway, mess that she was, when Daddy held out his hand.

"No, no, Hugh, I wouldn't—no need. You go on and hop back to bed now, Julia, and I'll bring in your dinner—"

"You mean, I can't eat with the rest of you?" Julia's voice soared way up with disappointment. Not to eat with everyone when Uncle Hugh was here! Not fair!

"Oh, ur-rk!" said Greg, pretending to be sick.

"Hello, Hugh," said Mama, and she put her arms around his neck and gave him a good, firm kiss on the cheek and patted his shoulder as if she were comforting him or something. At least that was the way her voice sounded. A special sort of voice.

And then here was Gramma, coming in wiping her hands on her apron, and Uncle Hugh went over and gave her a hug. "*Well,*" said Gramma, "what a fine how-do-you-do it all is, isn't it! Celia told me." Just for a second Julia thought Gramma meant about the poison oak being a fine how-do-you-do, but then she saw

everybody looking at everybody else, and their eyebrows going up and Greg was staring at the carpet and
running the heel of one shoe around a design, so that
she had the queerest feeling they weren't talking about
her poison oak at all.

"What's the ma—?" she began, when Mama suddenly took her by the shoulder and urged her on her
way.

"Back to bed with you, Julia."

So she had her dinner on a tray on her lap, with
Patchy-cat beside her licking his chops from his own
dinner and neatening his glossy black fur with the
white spots on it, one on his back and a large patch on
his underside, and paying special attention to his ears.
But why did Daddy call Patchy's jaws his chops? Why
didn't he say "licking his mouth"? Sister was there on
Julia's bed, hugging her knees, and they told each
other Continued Stories the way they did every night
when the light was turned out.

When Uncle Hugh finally came in, he had two packages, and Greg was with him.

"Surprises, Julia," said Uncle Hugh, and she gave a
yip of excitement. When Greg unwrapped his package
it was a book about trains, full of fine, big colored
pictures, the one he'd been wanting ever since he'd
seen it in a bookstore window. And for Julia there was
a book called *Just So Stories.* Uncle Hugh read one of
them aloud called "The Elephant's Child" about a

little elephant who had so much " 'satiable curtiosity"
that his family got fed up with him asking questions all
the time and spanked him.

"What's "satiable curtiosity,' Uncle Hugh?" asked
Julia.

Greg groaned and left, partly because Mama was
calling him to come and help clear up, but partly because Julia was asking another question. He always
groaned when Julia asked questions.

"It means," said Uncle Hugh, "it means '*in*satiable
curiosity.' The kind that never dies down. And that
little elephant was just like a certain person, full of
whats and wheres and whens and whys—"

"Oh," said Julia. "*Me.* Uncle Hugh, is Hulda all
right?"

Uncle Hugh, who had maybe been thinking about
nothing but little elephants full of 'satiable curtiosity
and certain people who were just like him, gave Julia
the same quick, startled look that Gramma had given
her when she asked about Uncle Hugh and Aunt Alex.
"Why-y, now—what makes you ask that?"

"I just wondered. She didn't hurt her leg, did she?"

"Hurt her leg!" he exclaimed. "Why on earth
would you think she'd done that? No, of course she
hasn't."

After Uncle Hugh had turned off the light and given
her a good-night kiss and gone out, Julia kept seeing
Hulda with her bandaged leg and the two of them

sitting in the little room on a train with a lot of other people. And then she'd lost Hulda—Hulda was left behind and the train swept on through strange country. It made Julia's heart beat hard all over again just to remember it—as if it had really happened. But it hadn't, had it?

She flopped over on one side, then the other, but couldn't go to sleep. What she wanted was a drink, so she got up and went down the hall to the living room, where she could hear everybody talking. And just as she opened the door to ask Mama, she heard Uncle Hugh say, "But I can't now, Celia. I refuse to, until she says it's all forgotten. It's so wrong—so unfair. To make an innocent person, who's been doing her level best to give good service, feel like that. It makes me so angry, I—"

At that moment Mama saw Julia at the door and put up her hand so that Uncle Hugh stopped talking and he didn't say another word while Mama got the glass of water. Then Julia said good-night all over again to everybody, trying to linger, but Mama shooed her away.

6

The Old Witch

"Maisie gives me a pain in my bellyache," said Julia.

And the reason for this was that Maisie would come over to see if they could get on with their checker games, having a tournament the way Daddy had shown them, when Maisie got home from school in the afternoons. But each time Julia went to the door, Maisie would take one look at her, see that she still had her bandages on with the yellow places on them, and say, "Oh, *ick!*" And she'd turn up her nose and wouldn't come in because, she said, she didn't want to touch a thing that Julia had. Neat and clean as when she'd started out for school in the morning, her hair drawn smoothly back into two pigtails with a little ribbon on the end of each of them, she'd twirl around, pigtails flying out, and skip down the steps again as she'd done every day this week. And Julia felt exactly what Greg said she was—a *mess.*

"Ridiculous!" said Mama about Maisie. "Why does she come over at all—?"

But finally Julia's poison oak dried up—no more lotion, no more bandages—and she could go back to school with her hair brushed and a dress on instead of her "everlasting old coveralls," as Gramma called them, that Julia loved best. And one afternoon when Julia and Maisie were playing checkers, getting on with their tournament in Julia's room, here came Brucie Clemens from down the street, slipping in from the garden through the French doors. Maisie had just drawn a fourth line at the end of a row of three under "Maisie" on their score sheet. Julia had two lines—she usually had less than Maisie.

"Can we play doctor under the house?" Brucie wanted to know.

Brucie was only five, but he was a good, obedient patient when Julia and Maisie wanted to take turns being doctor and nurse. They could give him lemon juice to make him better, and he would take it, even though he had to wrinkle up his face to swallow it. And he didn't mind having his temperature taken with a twig in his mouth, or being operated on. And he'd yell and carry on something fierce at all the right times.

"Let me be doctor now," he said once, when he finally thought it could be his turn. But both Julia and

Maisie said he was too young. He wouldn't know how to be doctor. Well, could he be nurse, then? But they said that boys weren't ever nurses, only girls. So he was stuck with being what he was.

Now Julia clapped the checkerboard closed, glad as anything that Brucie had come, with Maisie winning four games in a row. They went around to the side of the house where there was a little low door that led down a few steps to the gloomy basement, though it wasn't really much of a basement. There was barely room for Daddy to stand up in, so all he kept in it, near the door, was some old lumber and a stack of wood for the fireplace. Julia and Maisie had put a board on two boxes, which was Brucie's hospital bed. And he'd just given out a series of terrible, long drawn-out groans, and was tossing and turning on his bed of pain, when the low doorway, that had let the rays of the westering sun into their dim cave, darkened. Julia was telling Brucie to lie still or he'd only make things worse.

"What's all this again—*what's* all this, now!" came a harsh, accusing voice that Julia knew only too well. It belonged to the woman, Mrs. Weed, who was someone Mama called a landlady, though what that was, Julia didn't know. "Come out of there at *once,* you wicked children. What are you *do*ing to that poor little boy? I won't *have* such goings-on under the house, as I've told you quite clearly before, Julia Redfern. Now, I never, never want you under here again!"

There was a moment of silence while the children peered at the face glaring in at them. Then one by one they went up the stairs, out into the light of day, and Brucie scuttled home. But Maisie stood looking up at Mrs. Weed in her pot hat that was pulled low to just above her eyes. As usual, she had on her old brown coat with the thin fur around her neck fastened by a beady-eyed animal's head, narrow like a tiny fox's or weasel's, whose jaws bit its own tail, which was the other end of the fur. And she had a large, worn old purse that she held up in front of her just below her chest.

"Are you some relative of Julia's?" asked Maisie. "Are you her aunt?"

"No, I am not Julia's aunt, Miss Inquisitive. I own this house and I've come here to see your mother, Julia. Is she at home?"

At this very moment, Mama, who had just returned from work, came out onto the front porch. "Who is it, Julia?" she called. And when Julia and Maisie and Mrs. Weed came around, "Oh, Mrs. Weed," she said, and Julia knew instantly, by the dying-out tone of her voice, that she wasn't happy to see her. "Won't you come in?"

"Indeed I will," said Mrs. Weed firmly. "We have some business to discuss." And she came up the steps, not forgetting to pause and stare at the hump in the front walk, where roots were pushing up underneath, that Daddy had said he would surely get at one of these days.

Maisie came on in, too, but Mama was so taken up with Mrs. Weed's arrival that she didn't seem to notice.

"Yes, Mrs. Weed," said Mama when they were all settled in the living room.

"*Well,*" said Mrs. Weed, "I see you've been a-painting and all."

"Yes. The old wallpaper up there above the paneling was terribly faded, and even coming loose in places. So we just took it off and painted. And we polished the paneling and cleaned the bricks of the fireplace, as you can see."

"Well, I must say I could have done with a different color of paint, *if* I'd been asked, which I wasn't," said Mrs. Weed, turning her head this way and that.

"But we thought," said Mama, "that the soft gold would be rich and light, and yet not too bright in this rather shadowy room. What color would you have liked?"

"Well, a nice tan would have been my choice. But it's too late now—and it doesn't matter one way or the other. Painting isn't what I'm calling about, even though I did see Mr. Redfern in his old paint overalls out in the garden once or twice, so I had a notion what was going on. What I've come to say is—I've decided to sell the place."

Mama didn't seem able to speak for a second or two. Then she put her hands up to her chin, palms together, the way she always did, Julia had noticed, when she was struck by something.

"Oh, Mrs. Weed, *are* you?" she said in a low voice. "But you know my husband and I want the house, and I understood you to agree we could buy it later on. I had no idea you were thinking of selling. And we *will* buy it—not just immediately, it's true, but that's why we painted—every room, the kitchen and everything."

"Well, *I* certainly wasn't aware of any agreement on *my* part that you were going to buy it. But, in any case, I've no time to fuss around," Mrs. Weed said briskly. "I'm planning to move out of town and I need the cash —not just a down payment." She studied Mama for a moment and then stood up to go. "I just wanted to let you know so you could start hunting for another place. I've got the For Sale sign in my car, and I'll be bringing people to look." She moved to the door, and Mama got up in silence and went along after her.

Pretty soon, when Mrs. Weed had gone out to her car and come back again, she could be seen digging a hole just outside the fence with a gardening trowel. She stuck the spiked end of the For Sale sign into it, thumped the top of the sign good and hard with the trowel handle, and tamped the soil down all around the spike by stamping on it with her heel. Then she went to her car, tossed the trowel onto the seat, got in, and drove away.

Mama and Julia stood on the front porch watching, but the minute Mrs. Weed had gone out to her car, Maisie had skipped home. And in a while, after Mrs. Weed had driven off, back she came with her mother.

"Oh, Mrs. *Red*fern," cried Mrs. Woollard, shaking her head with indignation, "and after all the work you and Mr. Redfern put in on this house—doing all that painting and cleaning the brick. I never heard of such a thing! You know why she's decided to sell? Because she knew you and Mr. Redfern were doing all that fixing up, *that's* why. She drove by and saw Mr. Redfern in his overalls bringing in his paint buckets and the ladder from the garage the way I did. She's just taking advantage of you, that's what she's doing, selling while the house is all newly done up, I'll wager anything. Going out of town, my foot!"

"She's an old witch, that's what she is!" shouted Julia. "She's a mean old witch—"

"Hush, Julia," said Mama sharply. "Of course she's not a witch. A landlady has a perfect right to sell her own house—"

"I'm glad nobody can sell *our* house," said Maisie with huge satisfaction.

"And what makes you think nobody can, young one?" demanded Mrs. Woollard, giving Maisie a stern, sidelong look. "The landlord could sell any time, just like Mrs. Weed."

"But *why?*" exclaimed Maisie, her face going even paler than usual with shock and embarrassment, her big dark eyes sparkling. "It's our house—"

"Oh, no, it is *not* our house, Maisie. The landlord owns it, and because he owns it, he's the landlord and can do with it what he wants. If he decided to sell it, we'd have to move out, too. So don't you be so quick and smart about things."

Maisie stared at her mother, then quickly at Julia. "I don't *believe* it!" And she turned and leaped down the stairs, flew along the walk, and across the street and home. And banged the door behind her.

Ha-ha, said Julia inside herself. So there, Miss Maisie Smarty Woollard.

But Mrs. Woollard was going on again, saying that unless Mama asked Gramma to come and stay during the day while everybody was away and Mrs. Weed came with her lookers, those lookers would be into all the closets and drawers and nosing into everything that was none of their business. That was what lookers always did, she said, whether they had any intention of buying or not. And it made Julia so mad she could have exploded.

7

Up at the Park

So all the next week Gramma came first thing every morning so she could keep an eye on Mrs. Weed and the lookers throughout the day, and then stayed to dinner so she could tell Mama and Daddy and Greg and Julia what had happened. Gramma's eyes sparked with a mixture of malice and pleasure as she told all about the goings-on. If there was one person she couldn't abide, she said, it was "that Mrs. Weed," and not because she was a landlady—Gramma knew several decent ones—but just because she was Mrs. Weed, a particular kind of person.

"You should just hear her talking about how clean and fresh everything is—newly painted, she says all the time, as if *she'd* had it done *and* paid for it! And believe you me, I spoke up the first time she had a couple here, and when she said that about everything being so fresh and all, I said, yes, my daughter and son-in-law did it only a month or so ago, themselves, at their own expense. *Oh!*" exclaimed Gramma, her eyebrows dancing up and down, "if that didn't make Mrs. W furious. Her face got all red, especially her nose, and she said, *well,* of course, she'd asked so little rent it was no wonder her tenants wanted to keep the place nice.

"And I said, well, I knew the rent was about as usual, just about what you'd expect. So she hurried the man and his wife on into the next room, and the next time she came around she said, just as sweet as honey, that she didn't want to interrupt me at my work, and that I needn't trouble to go around with them—she could take care of her people as they went through.

"And I said nobody was troubling me in the slightest, and I stuck to 'em like sticky paper. And she kept staring at me as if she could have poked me, and then she'd smile and smile whenever one o' the lookers asked her a question. And I'd get each of the lookers aside, sooner or later, and tell 'em how my daughter and son-in-law had done all the painting and cleaning up, and not a penny paid for it, but told to get out as soon as they'd finished—"

"Oh, Mother, you didn't!" exclaimed Mama, but there was a quirk at the corner of her mouth, and Daddy and Greg let out barks of laughter. Julia just sat there, quiet, enjoying Gramma's telling, and feeling triumphant, in spite of everything, to think of Mrs. Weed's fury.

But none of Gramma's remarks did the least bit of good, because on Saturday Mrs. Weed phoned early, just as Mama was about to set out to hunt for something, an apartment, or a house if she could find one. A man had bought the place, Mrs. Weed said, and so she was giving the Redferns a month's notice.

"Oh, and I thought," said Mama, putting down the phone, "that if nobody bought right away, maybe I'd have a good while to hunt for something weekends. Because I do want a house and not an apartment, *and* with a fireplace, *and* with a garden—like this one."

"Celia," said Daddy, "don't hope for so much, then you won't be disappointed. We were very lucky to get a place like this. Would you like me to come with you?"

"No," sighed Mama, "what would be the use? One can hunt as well as two. You might just as well stay here and get on with your writing while you have the chance, because pretty soon we'll have to start packing," and she picked up her purse and went on her way.

Right after lunch Greg said he was going up to the park, because Bob had to have his hair cut that afternoon. Instantly, Julia got an idea. She and Greg were wiping the dishes while Daddy washed, and as soon as he was finished and had gone back into the bedroom and was clacking away at his typewriter, Julia got hold of Greg.

"Greg," she said in a low voice, "I have a secret to show you up at the park. Mama wouldn't believe me when I told her, but then she wouldn't go and look where it is. It's im*por*tant—"

"Ho, important!" scoffed Greg. "What's up there that's so important?"

"I don't want to tell you until you see it. Then you'll know I'm right—and you can go and play with the kids as soon as I've shown you, and I'll come back."

Greg looked so scornful and disbelieving that Julia was scared he was going to get on his bike and zip up without her. But he must have been feeling kindly for some strange reason, because he waited at the end of each block for her—with her box and her two big spoons, which she wouldn't explain about—until they got to the park. When he'd put his bike with the others, Julia led him across the grass, not to the steep part of the canyon where the poison oak was, but a good bit farther down toward the foot of the park where the creek meandered under a tall wire fence into somebody's back garden.

"Look!" she said, kneeling on the bank of the creek and pointing at the glistening specks of gold that lay on the bottom, gathered into little hollows where the water was quiet, or slipping and gliding where it moved faster.

"What?" said Greg, staring into the water. "I don't see anything—"

"But the gold, Greg, the *gold!* Don't you *see* it?"

"That? Oh, for the love of Mike, I might have known. That's fool's gold—"

"Not real gold?"

"Real gold! How could it be real gold, lying right there for everybody to see and nobody scooping it out. It's iron pyrites or maybe copper pyrites. And it's always been called fool's gold, so you're a fool like all the rest in the old days who were panning for gold and thought this was it."

"I am *not* a fool. You're so smart—you always think you know everything."

"Well, I know a heck of a lot more than a little kid like you," said Greg, poking around in the creek, trying to catch the tiny fish that darted past his fingers. "I know something special."

"*What* something special that I don't?" demanded Julia, stung by her same old jealousy at Greg's being let into affairs she was too young for.

"I know a secret," said Greg quietly, sitting back on his heels and studying her.

"Bet you don't. *What* secret?"

"Well, if it's a secret, I can't tell you, can I?" Oddly, though, instead of getting right up and going off to

play with the other boys, who were kicking their football around again, he sat there staring at her, yet not really seeing her, as if he were thinking. Then he seemed to come to and began stabbing at the grass with a stick and drawing it back and forth. And somehow Julia knew, just as clear as clear could be, that he was bursting to tell her. So she kept quiet, because if she said the wrong thing he might change his mind. It was a very chancy moment. But pretty soon he looked up and said, "It's about Uncle Hugh and Aunt Alex."

"It *is*? *What*, Greg—*what*?" She remembered Mama talking on the phone to Uncle Hugh that night she first had poison oak. And then later, when Uncle Hugh came over to dinner and brought the books, he'd stopped talking the minute she'd come in and asked for a drink. She'd felt both times that something was wrong, that something was brewing.

"Well," said Greg with enormous gravity, "Uncle Hugh and Aunt Alex have had a big blowup—"

"How do you know? How do you *know* that?"

"Oh, I just do. And it's about Hulda."

"About Hulda—but why?"

"Because Aunt Alex thinks Hulda broke something, and Hulda says she didn't, but Aunt Alex kept acting so funny because she said she knew perfectly well that bottle hadn't been broken when she last put it down in the morning, and there it was in the evening, cracked, and the top of it broken. And nobody could have done it but Hulda, dusting up there—and that's exactly what Hulda *had* been doing. Aunt Alex went around all quiet and wouldn't say anything, and so Hulda left because she couldn't stand being suspected. And Uncle Hugh was mad as blazes because he says he knows—he absolutely *knows*—that Hulda would never do a thing like that and not tell Aunt Alex.

"But Aunt Alex can't find one of her rings and she saw a chipped glass in the closet, a goblet or something, one of her crystal ones that Hulda said was chipped when she came. That's why Aunt Alex let Mrs. Mason go, because she was always chipping everything. So Hulda's gone to stay with her sister, and Uncle Hugh's at some hotel. He had an awful big blowup with Aunt Alex, but I bet partly because she's so bossy. Maybe he got fed up. Anyway, he wants Aunt Alex to phone Hulda and say everything's all right, but she won't. She's staying with friends for a visit."

Julia had gone all hollow inside, and felt so sick she thought she might be going to throw up. She was kneeling, drooped over and staring at the grass but not seeing it. The only thing she could see were the two halves of the little animal lying there on the glass of Aunt Alex's dressing table, and then her own hands coming out and putting the two halves back together and slipping them, as if they were one whole piece again, into the neck of the bottle. And then putting the bottle very carefully back among the other little bottles sitting in a crowd under the big mirror.

She could remember the faint smell of the perfume,

even now, like apple blossoms, Mama said it was. The
fragrance and the small broken animal. And the soft
light and cool quiet air of Aunt Alex's beautiful bedroom. And then tiptoeing quietly out, very, very quietly. And not telling anybody.

"What kind of a bottle, Greg?"

"Oh, one of Aunt Alex's silly little perfume bottles
that she's got millions of. And not the whole bottle
broken, either. It was just cracked, and the top was
broken. What a fuss about nothing. Though Aunt Alex
said it was an heirloom, a real museum piece, very old.
And priceless."

Silence. So then the bottle had gotten cracked, as
well as the top broken. "What's a 'air loom'?" asked
Julia in a faint, queer voice.

"Oh, something handed down in the family. Aunt
Alex said it was her grandmother's—or maybe her
great-grandmother's." Julia sat there not saying anything, so Greg got up. "Well, you go on home now.
And if you tell my secret, remember I'll cut you up into
little bits. So don't say a *word.*"

8

Daddy

Daddy was sitting quiet in his room, and when the front door closed, "That you, Julia? Or is it Celia?"

"It's me, Daddy." Again, Julia's voice sounded small and strange and far away, but Daddy didn't seem to notice, because he started right in typing again. So Julia went to her room, and there on her bed were Patchy-cat and Sister and a sheet of paper with typing on it. Julia stood looking down at it, still feeling so hollow and sick she didn't know what she was going to do with herself. Then she picked it up—it was a poem, and she knew of course that Daddy had written it. The poem was called "When Unicorn Comes" and right under the title it said "(For Julia)," just like that, her name between two little curved lines. And this was the poem:

For us, for otter, badger,
Squirrel and hare,
Fox, mountain lion,
And great brown bear,
Unicorn bows his head,
And his glimmering horn,
Powerful as no other
And white as he,
Ruffles the poisoned brook—
And now damselfly and furred
    bronze bee,
Kingfisher, ouzel, woodthrush and tit
Dip down, and we as well
Drink cool and deep and free,
And cannot have enough of it:
Sweet water, clear water, moving over
    tawny stone,
Reflecting pale horn of Unicorn,
Otter's face, badger's, squirrel's
    and hare's,
Fox's, mountain lion's, and great
    brown bear's.

Julia sank onto her bed, still holding the page, and she felt so sad she didn't even want to cry. She knew why Daddy had written this poem. He'd read her and Greg a story about Unicorn the other night, how the huntsmen were trying to kill it with their arrows, but it ran and laid its head in the lap of the Lady, and because she was pure, Unicorn was safe. He could touch his horn to any poisoned food or drink and drive away the poison so that the food wouldn't hurt anyone or make them sick or kill them, because his horn was magical.

Sister didn't need to ask Julia what the matter was. She knew. "Poor Julia," she said. And Patchy-cat looked up at her from out of his tail where it was curled around over his hind legs and said "Ah-ah-ah?" by way of greeting. Then he blinked and yawned so hugely, it was a wonder, Mama would say, that his jaws didn't come unhinged. Then he unwound himself and stretched and stretched until he quivered. Julia leaned over and buried her face in his soft, clean, specially Patchy-cat-smelling stomach fur where it was warm from being closed in while he slept. She loved the smell of Patchy-cat, his sleepy-warm underfur, or the smell of him when he'd been in the cold, damp grass all night, or when he'd been in the dry, fragrant weeds of summer fields, tracking after mice. "Patchy, Patchy!" and he said "Ah-ah-ah" again and laid his paw across her face.

But there was no comfort anywhere. This was the worst fix she'd ever been in—a terrible fix she could see no way out of. How could she tell anyone what she'd done after the awful things that had happened, Hulda leaving Aunt Alex and Uncle Hugh and refusing to come back until Aunt Alex phoned her to. But she never would. *Never.* Not Aunt Alex. And then she and Uncle Hugh having their blowup. "Oh, Patchy, Patchy!"

Julia lay on her bed beside him, with Sister on her other side, and knew that Daddy wanted her to come in to him. She had this funny little feeling that told her he did. But, why, when he was typing away in there and didn't ever like to be interrupted when he was writing. All the same, she had to go. She knew that.

She got up and went along the hall past the bathroom to the door of the living room and stood there and listened. Daddy wasn't typing. He was waiting for her. So she went across to the door of his and Mama's bedroom and all the time her heart was thudding and thudding like something trapped in her chest, wanting to get out. And she still had the hollow, sick feeling in her middle, yet she had to go in.

"Hello, Julia," said Daddy. He held out an arm and she went to him and he drew her up onto his lap. "Are you all right?" he asked.

Slowly, Julia shook her head, but couldn't manage to say anything, not right away. He waited, and pretty soon, almost in a whisper, "I found my poem you wrote."

"And did you read it—did you like it?"

"Yes—yes, I do. I know why you wrote it. Because of the story."

"That's right." Again he waited, and when Julia said nothing more, "Do you have something to tell me?"

She swallowed, her face buried against his chest. Then she took a deep breath. "Daddy?"

"Yes—"

"I broke the little animal."

"The little animal?" He sounded completely puzzled.

"Yes," she whispered, "the little animal on top of the bottle."

"Julia, I can't hear you." And he leaned his head down.

"On top of the bottle—the part that goes in. Aunt Alex's bottle that's a air loom."

Daddy was still for a moment, then he sighed. "But when, Julia? How did it happen?"

"Uncle Hugh was in the bathroom, so I went upstairs to go to the other one, but I went into Aunt Alex's bedroom first, for just a second. And I picked up the bottle—"

"And that was when it happened," said Daddy. "You dropped it."

"Yes. So then I went downstairs, quick, to the bathroom down there because Uncle Hugh was through, and then we went."

Daddy sat thinking, both arms around her, his chin resting on the top of her head. "You know," he said at length, "I can't for the life of me understand why

no one's suspected you. It seems never to have oc-
curred to any of them that you'd been upstairs. No one
has so much as mentioned *you,* only Hulda." He was
quiet again, and then, "Well, Julia"—and he slipped
her onto her feet with his hands on her shoulders—
"we've got to do something about Hulda, haven't we?
And at once—before she takes a job with some other
family. *If* she can get one, because she'll have no references—"

"What's those?"

"References? A letter that says that Hulda Holgerson has been a good and faithful housekeeper and a
first-rate cook, and is absolutely honest and trust-
worthy." Oh my, thought Julia despairingly, Aunt
Alex would never write that now. "So what we must
do is phone Hulda's sister, and go over and see them
so you can tell Hulda what happened. I don't think the
sister lives too far away from here. Didn't you and
Mama go and see them two or three times when Hulda
was there?"

"Yes," said Julia. "We went to have tea with them
—at least Mama did. I had milk and cookies—they
were awfully good. And Mama and I took the Dwight
Way Dinky."

"I see." By the Dwight Way Dinky, Julia meant the
little streetcar, rather like one of the San Francisco
cable cars but much smaller, that went swaying and
bouncing back and forth along Dwight Way and that

everybody joked about even though they were fond of it. "Well, we'll have to look up Hulda's sister's phone number. What's her married name?"

Julia looked at Daddy blankly. *She* didn't know.

"Well, what do you call her? Mrs. what?"

"I call her Mrs. Anna—Hulda said I could. Is that her married name?"

"No, no," said Daddy, "that's her first name. So we're stopped in our tracks right there. But I'll tell you what. We'll hop on the Dinky and go over anyway. And if they're not at home, we'll leave a note to call us. Go and get into a dress, now, and put on some clean socks and decent shoes, and we'll be there in twenty minutes. Seems to me Mama said the sister lives on Laurel, right near Dwight. Would you recognize the house?"

Of course she would, Julia said, and was halfway across the living room when the postman came, but he didn't shove the letters through the slot as he usually did. He rang the doorbell and Julia was about to go, but Daddy went instead. When she came back after a little in a clean dress, Daddy was in his room again.

She looked in and he was sitting there at his desk reading one of his stories. The top of the big tan envelope, tossed down on the rug, had been torn open, so it was a story that had come back from whatever magazine he'd sent it to. The magazine didn't want it. He was sitting with his forehead resting on one hand while he read the story over, but in the midst of his reading he looked up and stared at the wall, then said to himself, low and intense, "But it's good—it's *good. I know* it is—" And he let the story slide and put his head in his hands and just sat there.

"Daddy?" said Julia. He didn't seem to hear, and for some reason she was frightened of him when he was like this. Perhaps not frightened exactly, but she had no idea how to speak to him or what to say. He was different, dark, all closed up, when his stories came back from places that didn't want them. She was happy and at ease with him at other times, but now she felt as if he'd gone away from her. Suddenly he got up and walked past as if he didn't see her and went out the front door. She knew what would happen. He'd go for a long, long walk and not come back until maybe dinnertime.

But he'd *said* they must go and see Hulda. She must tell Hulda what she'd done so everything would be all right. She sat down in the living room to wait and see if Daddy would come back, but he didn't. So she looked in her purse that Aunt Alex and Uncle Hugh had given her, and there was a nickel and three dimes and some pennies. Why shouldn't she go anyway and surprise him—and Mama. *And* Greg! Daddy would be proud of her that she'd gone on her own. It wasn't much farther than going to school, and she was sure she remembered Hulda's sister's house.

She went out onto the front porch and then thought about Maisie. What if Maisie was watching and wondered where she was going, all by herself and dressed up like this? She'd come skimming across the street and yell, "Where'ya going, Julia—where's your mama?" And Julia wouldn't tell Maisie for anything, because Maisie would ask why she was going by herself.

She'd skip along asking questions all the way to the end of the block and maybe even to Dwight Way, because that was the next block after. And because Julia would say to mind her own business, she'd run right back home and tell her mother that Julia was up to something and wouldn't tell what. And that she'd gotten on the Dwight Way Dinky all by herself! But *that*, thought Julia, wasn't anything much. Lots of schoolkids did, even little ones.

Julia sneaked along behind the blackberry vines and found her special escape place onto the street that Maisie couldn't see from her house. She got through without tearing her dress and was running along Brucie Clemens's block so Maisie wouldn't catch her going down their own street toward Dwight Way when who should pop out from the bushes but Brucie.

"Julia, Julia!" he cried, hopping up and down with excitement, "can we play doctor under the house, and can I be—?"

"No," Julia flung back over her shoulder. "I'm busy.

Little *kids!*" she muttered to herself in disgust and ran on. When she got to Dwight Way, she was just in time to catch the Dinky going in the right direction, and the conductor leaned down to help her clamber up the steep, narrow steps.

He was a small, stout man who was one of two always up front running the streetcar, sitting on his tall stool, and collecting the money. It was dropped into a coin box, and went down a jointed shoot that you could see through, inside the glass part of the box. If there wasn't too much, so that the money got clogged, it went on down into the metal part. And every once in a while the conductor would turn a little wheel with a handle at the side of the box, very fast, around and around and around, to get all the money down. And the sound it made, Julia thought, was *clebney-clebney-clebney-cliff, clebney-cliff.* But she'd never told anybody this. She'd never thought to tell anybody, or how much she longed to turn that little wheel herself.

"Aren't you with anybody, girlie?" asked the conductor. "Where's your mama?"

"Oh, she's busy," said Julia. "I'm going to see a friend. How much shall I put in?" and she held out her palm with the nickel and three dimes and the pennies on it. She thought a dime, and sure enough the conductor took up a dime and dropped it in the box.

"How far ye going?"

"Laurel," said Julia, "where Hulda lives. Will you

tell me when we get there?" She'd heard Mama ask this of the conductor sometimes.

He nodded and she went and sat down inside. She wasn't sure about sitting on one of the outside seats facing the street, which were so close to the edge that Julia thought she might tip off because the Dinky bounced so. She and Mama always sat outside and Julia wasn't scared then. It was fun, jouncing and leaning against each other, sometimes overcome with giggles because the Dinky was just like the Toonerville Trolley in the funny paper.

"Aspen," sang out the conductor. Somebody got off, and then it was Oak and Elm and Pine and Deodar and Eucalyptus, and more people got on and off. Then "Laurel!" called out the conductor and waggled a finger to Julia. She got up, feeling rather elderly, holding her purse with her money in it as if she did this by herself every day of her life. She hopped down the steps and waved to the conductor. "See you on your way back, young lady. You be careful, now—" She called up to him that she would. "Have a good time," he said, and the Dinky swayed and rattled away.

9

Real or Dream?

Julia ran over to the sidewalk and looked around. At once she knew with a dreadful sinking feeling that she hadn't been paying any attention when she and Mama had come to Hulda's sister's house those other times. She had a sort of picture of the house in her mind, but now she knew that she wasn't in the least certain of just what she and Mama had done. Had they gone on along Laurel straight from where the Dinky stopped, or crossed the tracks and gone the other way? She couldn't be sure. She turned around in a circle and then went along Laurel straight from where she'd gotten off, looking at the houses on each side of the street, watching for Mrs. Anna's.

She walked along and along, came to the end of the

block, crossed over, and kept walking. Had she and
Mama come this far? She didn't think so, but kept on,
puzzled and unhappy. She had been walking for four
blocks when all at once a bunch of kids came zooming
around the corner on skates and smacked into her.
Down she went on her elbow, skidding along the sidewalk, and the chain handle of her purse slid right out
of her hand.

"Hey," yelled the boy who had knocked her down,
"why'n't ye look where ye're going!" And he snatched
up her purse, jiggled it and heard the money, opened
it and shook the two dimes and the nickel and the
pennies onto his hand. "Well, *what* about that—!" He
stared at them for a second, glanced up grinning, then
shoved them into his pocket.

"You better not, Stuey," warned one of the others,
but the rest jeered at the warning boy, and another
grabbed the purse out of Stuey's hand and scrounged
around in it himself to see if there were any more coins
inside.

Julia had gotten up, her elbow and arm stinging like
fury as if they had been burned, and she was in a rage
and flew at the boy with her purse. "That's *my* purse
and you *give* it to me!" she shouted. She pummeled
him with her fists so that he wobbled, trying to keep
himself upright, and snatched her purse back. Then
she turned on the one who'd taken her money, but he
was laughing at her, and when she ran at him, her head

down, he simply swatted her aside with one arm and
sent her sprawling again. Then off they went on their
skates, so fast that by the time Julia had gotten to her
feet, she knew she could never catch up with them.

Her money was gone, all she had, so how could she
get home if she couldn't find Mrs. Anna's house?

Quietly she sniffled to herself as she held on to her
bloody, burning arm and went on along the street. But
at least she had her purse, she thought, even though
the chain had snapped when she'd grabbed it from the
second boy. But all her beautiful money! She looked
down and saw blood all over the front of her good
dress. What would Mama say? That she should never
have started out for Mrs. Anna's house by herself when
she wasn't really sure where it was. But she *had* been
sure—absolutely sure! Until she got off the Dinky.
And she'd so much wanted to surprise everybody.

She kept walking and walking, blocks and blocks, it
seemed, and crossed a very busy street that she thought
surely she had seen before. Suddenly she stopped in
the middle of the sidewalk and asked herself: But am
I going in the right direction? For some reason, she
wasn't sure. Being knocked into by the boys had
turned her around. She looked up at the street sign and
it didn't say Laurel, but Dickens, and the other way it
said 2nd. *There wasn't any Laurel.* Was this dreaming
or real?

Now it was all too much like something else that had

happened to her—somewhere, sometime, some terrible time, when she was banging on a door that had closed her away from Hulda. The train was speeding faster and faster, leaving Hulda behind, and Julia didn't know where she was or where she was going.

She walked on and on, desolate and terror-stricken, sobbing aloud. Once she and Mama and Daddy and Greg had gone to the big Central Market over in Oakland, which was such a huge place it took ages and ages to work your way through it, through the crowds, from one end to the other. There were booths along the sides of the aisles with all kinds of food being sold, fruits and vegetables and meat, peanut butter and pickles and cheeses, and fresh bread and cakes and pies and all sorts of things to drink. The smells were mouthwatering. Julia was taking it all in, not paying any attention to Daddy, when somehow she lost hold of his hand and got all mixed up in the crowd, went down the wrong aisle, and couldn't find her family no matter how she yelled and shouted.

Finally she set up a great wail, so that somebody took her to the center of the market where lost children were to stay until their parents came for them. And Daddy and Mama and Greg *did* come for her, and when Daddy picked her up, she grabbed him so hard around the neck, "I thought you were going to choke me, Julia," he laughed. But he had a good grip of her hand after that and never let go once.

But now Daddy was far off somewhere and there was nowhere to go and wait so that he could come and find her. Oh, the sickness and desolation of being lost! She let out an especially loud sob and looked up, and what should she see but the Dinky going back the way it had come. She couldn't believe it. Surely it couldn't be *her* Dinky, because it was in the wrong place and it had a long way to go before it came back again, Mama said. Maybe this was *another* Dinky.

Then she noticed that two ladies had gotten off and were coming briskly in her direction, one plump and short and the other thin and short. Julia let out a shriek of joy and went careening toward them.

"*Hulda, Hulda*—Mrs. *Anna!*" She flung herself into the arms of the speechless Hulda and clung to her. "I got lost, Hulda—I got lost. I was on the wrong street and"—she stopped and hauled up a deep breath—"and I don't know how I'm here, back where I got off the Dinky—and those boys knocked me down and one of them took my money—"

"But, Julia," cried Hulda, "why are you here all by yourself? And look at your—"

"Yust look at your dress, Yulia—and your arm," exclaimed Mrs. Anna, who had come over from Sweden some time after Hulda and so still said *Y* for *J*. And though she was plump, she got down on one knee beside Julia, dropping all her packages. "*Look* at that child's arm—oh, those mean, wicked chudren!"

"Come, Anna," said Hulda, "let's get her home and
get that arm clean and bandaged and the blood out of
her dress. What will her mother say! The least we can
do is to get her cleaned up—" Mrs. Anna got to her
feet, Julia gathered the packages and away they hus-
tled with Julia between them, who was trying to ask
what happened to Laurel. Why had it disappeared?
The Dinky's conductor called out Laurel and Daddy
said they lived on Laurel. Was this it?

"It changes, Yulia," said Mrs. Anna.

"You mean like a troll into a dragon?"

"No," said Hulda. "Anna means that when it gets
to other side of First Street, it changes to Dickens,
which isn't very kind of it for people who don't know
that. Now let's get you all fixed up and then we'll hear
everything."

And right there at the end of the first block after you
got off the Dinky, Hulda and Mrs. Anna turned in
along a walk leading to a very small house buried
behind bushes and trees.

"So *this* is it," said Julia, "and I went right by it."

"Of course you did—so hidden it is." Mrs. Anna
went up onto the porch, dug into her purse for her key,
and let them in. A few minutes later Mrs. Anna had
slipped off Julia's dress and sponged out the blood on
the front of it, then took it into the sun to dry. Mean-
while Hulda was washing off her arm, then putting
peroxide on it, which made Julia screech and holler at

the sharp stinging, and to see the white foam bubble up all over the scraped, shiny red skin, and to smell the peculiar smell. Then once more she was bandaged, just like when she had poison oak, she told them.

"I think this is old Bandage Time," she said, looking down at Hulda's leg. However, Hulda's leg seemed to be as sturdy and smooth as always.

Not long after, they were all sitting in the little living room, which was stuffed with furniture, because Mrs. Anna and her husband had brought everything they owned with them from Sweden, but could afford only this small house. Julia was trying to explain about Daddy's story coming back in the mail after he was going to bring her here, and about his going off for a long walk by himself the way he always did when he was unhappy like that, but Julia knowing he wanted her to come to see Hulda because he'd said he did. And how she'd caught the Dinky without Maisie knowing a thing about it and then gotten off and walked and walked, feeling it was just like the train going away without Hulda.

"But *what* train, Yulia?" asked Mrs. Anna, completely puzzled.

"I don't know—but there was a train. Hulda, did you hurt your leg?"

"Hurt my leg, Julia?" repeated Hulda, staring at her. "Why, no, I haven't hurt myself at all."

"Then I don't understand. You could hardly walk and your leg was all done up."

"I never heard of such a thing!" cried Hulda. "I don't know what you're talking about, Julia. And this is the question. Why have you come? What made you go off without anyone knowing? Why did your father want to bring you here, and say you must come?"

Julia swallowed. Oh, yes, she'd told everything but that. (And there *was* something the matter with Hulda. She couldn't go back to Aunt Alex's.)

"Has Aunt Alex phoned yet, Hulda?"

Hulda and Mrs. Anna gazed at her. "No, your Aunt Alex hasn't phoned yet," said Hulda. "Did your mother tell you about what happened, Julia?"

There was a little tight silence while Julia stared down at the carpet and smoothed and smoothed her bandage. She was sitting on a stool facing Mrs. Anna and Hulda in their wing chairs. "Greg told me," she finally got out, "and that I mustn't say anything to anybody. But I have to tell you because there's something else—"

"Yes, Julia?" said Hulda.

"I broke the little animal. The magical animal, and when it came back together when I put it in the bottle again, I thought it was mended. I thought it would stay that way because it was magic—"

Hulda sighed, just the way Daddy had done when *he* was told. "Did you!" she said, shaking her head. "And you didn't say a word to anybody. Oh, Julia, dear—"

"But I thought it was *fixed*—" burst out Julia, and

she went blindly to Hulda and Hulda put her arms around her.

"Well," said Mrs. Anna, "so now it is all clear, and we will say no more about it. Yulia will tell her Uncle Hugh and Aunt Alex what happened and everything will be all right. Mrs. Alex can write a reference for Hulda after all, and she will get another good place."

But, "Oh, no, Anna," said Hulda.

There was another short tight silence. Julia rose up so that she could see what was going on, and saw that Mrs. Anna looked stunned with surprise and seemed not to know what to say.

"I don't want *another* good place," Hulda went on. "I want my good place with Mrs. Alex and Mr. Hugh. And I will get it, because Mrs. Alex wants me back. We don't even have to speak of Mr. Hugh—he'd have given me a reference at once if I'd wanted it, but I've never asked."

Mrs. Anna's round face had gone red with indignation, and her bright blue eyes, as bright and blue as Hulda's, snapped at Hulda. "Why, I'm yust a*maz*ed at you, Hulda Holgerson. To want to go back to that house after the way that woman—"

"*Anna!*" broke in Hulda. "Not a word—"

"But I don't care," cried Mrs. Anna, getting up out of her chair and walking up and down in her agitation. "You can't *do* this, Hulda! It isn't *right*. Where is your *pride*?"

Hulda laughed and laughed and leaned back in her chair. "Oh, Anna, do sit down. If everything is all right, because Julia has told the truth, and Mrs. Alex and Mr. Hugh both want me back and I want to go back—because I've never had such a good place—why shouldn't I go?"

"Because of the way that woman—I mean, because you weren't *trusted,* that's why!" exclaimed Mrs. Anna, stopping to stand in front of Hulda and Julia with her hands out. "And because she hasn't phoned you, even though she *does* want you back—*if* she does. And then it would yust be the same all over again next time— if anything happened, any little stupid thing, you'd be to blame."

"Oh, no, Anna. Never again. Mrs. Alex will never suspect me of anything again. You wait and see. She would be too ash— ah, well," and Hulda, having caught herself in the middle of a word, shrugged and chuckled. "Now, Anna, dear, what about something to celebrate?" She held out her hand to Mrs. Anna and Mrs. Anna took it, and slowly her round, pink face broke into a smile.

"Oh, Hulda," she said, "you're too good—too forgiving. But what can I do? You must go your own way, and I wish you well. Perhaps you are right—we shall see. And now I will heat the coffee cake and make coffee for us and chocolate for Yulia—"

"*Could* I have some?" exclaimed Julia. She found

she was starved, having been through so much. "Even though I—?"

"Yes," said Hulda, "even though you did the wrong thing, Julia. But you will undo it, even though we can't mend the little animal. And you still have the hardest part in front of you—telling Aunt Alex. And now I must phone your house to see if I can get some-one so that I can tell them where you are and that I'll be bringing you home in about half an hour."

Later, when she got on the Dinky again, this time with Hulda, Julia felt ever so much more elderly than the first time when she'd had her money and was being pleased with herself, traveling around as if she did it every day of her life. Now she felt positively ancient. And all at once, sitting there beside Hulda on an outside seat with her legs sticking straight out in front of her, something else came to mind. *What if Maisie found out?*

It didn't bear thinking about.

10

Just About Enough

But there was no getting away from Maisie. The instant Julia and Hulda came within sight of Maisie's house, there she was, racing toward them, an eager whirlwind bursting with news.

"Julia, Julia, your mother's been hunting all over for you—I told her when Mama and me were coming back from the grocery store we saw you going along the street all dressed up by yourself, and Mama told me to run after you and so I did, but you turned the corner and I couldn't catch up, and when I got around the corner I saw you get on the Dinky, so I told your Mama you got on, and was she ever *mad.* You better go right on in quick, Julia. Is this your aunt?"

"No, it isn't my aunt, Maisie Woollard. She's a friend of mind and I've been visiting—"

"What's the matter with your arm, Julia? Why've you got another bandage—have you got poison oak *again*—?"

"No, I have not got poison oak again. I fell down, and it's none o' your business."

Maisie's feelings weren't in the least hurt. Skipping and bobbing, pigtails flying with zesty liveliness, she was just about to slip inside too when they came to Julia's gate. But Julia quickly clicked it behind Hulda so that Maisie wouldn't follow.

"Hadn't I better come in, Julia?" Maisie wanted to know, hopping up on the lower crossbar, then hanging over the top of the gate and teetering.

"No, you can't," Julia shot back, going hot all over with anxiety. "You just stay right there. Hulda's company and we have to talk and you're *not allowed.* You go right back home—"

"Julia?" said Maisie. "You know after the mailman came? Well, I saw your papa go off in *that* direction, walking real fast. And I said hello to him, but he didn't answer. Is he mad at you? He *looked* mad, I told your mama. He hasn't come home yet."

"No, he's not mad." Julia came back along the walk and pushed Maisie off the gate. "I *told* you to go home—" She turned and ran along the walk again and up the steps to where Hulda was standing. But now Hulda, looking terribly embarrassed, suddenly started down.

Julia went to the door, which was standing halfway open, and there was Gramma, with her back to the porch, right inside, as if she'd been about to leave.

"—and if I've said it once, Celia, I've said it a hundred times," Gramma was going on, not very loud but easy to hear, "you spoil that man. You know you do, never asking him to do a single thing weekends, and taking his lunch in to him so he won't be disturbed while he stays stuck in that bedroom typing and leaving you to go off by yourself, *do* everything by yourself, and now this hunting for a place, all day long, and you working all week! Leaving him here, sitting in his comfort, taking his ease, and then going off without a note to you and leaving that child to disappear and you haven't any idea where. Well, it's a disgrace, that's what it is—" Gramma stopped to draw breath for a mere second, and in that second,

"Mother, I don't want to hear another word about Harry," said Mama in that quiet, firm, reaching voice of hers that Julia knew well from times when Mama was really angry, and that made Julia go all funny inside. "Not another word. I will do as I see fit about my own husband—"

"Oh, yes, *I* know, *I* know," said Gramma bitterly. "You always have. And I'm sticking my nose in where it's not wanted, even when I'm concerned about my own daughter. And so I'll go—" And she turned—and faced Julia and Hulda, and her dark little eyes widened with shock. But astonished as she must have been to see the two of them there together, and wondering how this could possibly have come about, she simply said, "So *there* you are, young lady. Hello, Hulda—" then brushed right past them and went tippeting down the steps with her string bag over her arm and her hat flat on her head. And out the gate, not even glancing back once (Maisie was by this time across at her own house, but watching), and hurried along the street, chin up.

"Mama?" called Julia. "Hulda's here." She pushed the door open a bit more and saw Mama come hastily forward.

Mama put her hand to her forehead and closed her eyes for a second. *"Julia,"* she said, "where in the name of heaven have you been, all dressed up? And bringing Hulda! What on earth got into you?" Then she held out her hands. "Hulda, dear—please come in. What an afternoon! Oh, I'm so glad to see the two of you, but I'm all at sixes and sevens. What could have made Julia— but come, now, let's sit down and get this all straightened out. Though what about tea? I'll go put the kettle on—" Because for Mama, when she was all at sixes and sevens, Julia knew, the only answer was a good, hot, strong cup of tea.

"No, no, Mrs. Redfern," said Hulda. "Julia and Anna and I have just had coffee cake and coffee—and Julia had cocoa. But please make yourself a cup. I think you need it—and I must tell you at once: I tried to get you twice on the phone, but no one was here, and so I asked Anna to phone you after we left."

"Oh, so it was Anna who was ringing. I was just coming in the door when it stopped—I haven't been home very long, only long enough to be clutched at by Maisie." Mama went out to the kitchen and ran water into the kettle, while Julia told Hulda which was Sister's chair.

"—that little heavy one with the fat arms and the fat back, just like a big chair. But she's not here now, Hulda, so I can sit in it. If she comes in, I'll get up and sit someplace else. She's probably in my bedroom—"

"Oh, I see," said Hulda, having looked a bit puzzled at first, but then nodding in understanding. "Sister—"

"Yes, we tell Continued Stories at night when we go to bed, and Patchy's there and sometimes the Japanese dolls, and it's nice. Mama"— and Julia twisted around when Mama came in—"Greg isn't back yet, is he?"

"Not that I know of. *Now,*" said Mama, sitting down, "I want to hear all about everything. That was very, very naughty of you, Julia, to go off without leaving me a note. In fact, it was *cruel* to go off where I couldn't find you, and especially on the Dinky."

"But Daddy told me we should go to see Hulda at Mrs. Anna's to tell her what happened about Aunt Alex's bottle so that Hulda wouldn't go to another family. So I went and got cleaned up, but when I came out again Daddy was saying things to himself about the story that came back, and so I waited to see what he'd do, but he just went out the door and I knew he was going for a walk. So I looked in my purse to see about money and there was enough, so I went and got on the Dinky because Daddy said Hulda would have to know. And I had to hurry because— Well, anyway," finished Julia faintly. "I didn't remember about leaving a note. I wanted it to be a surprise, about my telling Hulda—"

Mama studied Julia for a second or two in silence after Julia's voice had trailed away. She and Hulda were sitting on the couch facing Julia in Sister's chair. "About you telling Hulda *what?*" said Mama.

"About the little bottle. The magic animal on the top—"

Mama waited. "Well," she said, "go on."

"Well, you see"—and, oh, thought Julia, this was the worst yet, having to meet Mama's eyes, far, far worse, for some reason, than having to tell Daddy and Hulda—"you see, when I went upstairs because Uncle Hugh was in the other bathroom, I—I went into Aunt Alex's bedroom. And the little animal on top of the bottle fell and it—broke, but when I slid the top in, it was all together again, and I thought it was magic. That it was whole. And so I—just—put it back—"

"I see," said Mama slowly. "You just put it back

with all the other bottles and didn't say a word to anyone. Not to Uncle Hugh, nor to me, nor to Aunt Alex."

"But I thought it was *magic,* I told you—"

"No, you didn't, Jule," said Greg's voice, and he came in from the kitchen. "You just thought it was the easiest thing to think it was magic—the easiest way out, with nobody getting mad—"

"I *didn't*—I *didn't*—and you shut up, Greg Redfern," shouted Julia. "I always thought the little animal was magic. And it *was* whole, the top was. It was magicked whole, the minute I put it all back in again —the little animal did it."

"That will do, Julia and Greg," said Mama sharply, her voice trembling, because she was tired and fed up, Julia knew perfectly well. "I don't want to hear another word between the two of you—"

"Well, at least," muttered Greg, "I wouldn't kid myself."

"But I don't understand," said Mama, "how it all could have happened. Not one of us ever thought of you, Julia, and it was only Aunt Alex who thought of poor Hulda. You went inside, and then Uncle Hugh came out onto the porch and said to us that you'd be only a second, so he must have seen you—"

"Only coming back from the front door—"

"But what do you mean, coming *back* from the front door? You say Uncle Hugh was in the downstairs

bathroom and so you went upstairs. But when did Uncle Hugh see you coming in from the front door?"

"I don't remember," said Julia miserably. She was all mixed up. Oh, she knew what it would be the minute Greg got her alone. He wouldn't say much, but he'd look at her, doing his thinking. And he was going to cut her up into little bits for telling his secret.

But he'd already done some thinking, and he didn't seem to have his mind on cutting her up. "Now, Jule," he said, "what did you do the minute you got downstairs after you'd broken Aunt Alex's bottle?" and he plunked himself down on the floor, cross-legged, with his elbows resting on his knees. How he loved problems like this: figuring how mysteries could have happened, any kind of mystery. Daddy said he should be a detective.

"Well," said Julia, "when I came down, Uncle Hugh was in his study, right across from the bathroom. So I ran along the big hall toward the front door. I wasn't going to bother—"

"You mean you didn't want him to see you—you felt guilty, so what's all this about magic? You wanted to get outside just as fast as possible so nobody'd think you had time to go upstairs. Isn't that right?" pressed Greg sternly like a lawyer. Julia stared at him, the corners of her mouth drawn down and her chin up—her stubborn look, Mama called it. He had her on the hook and she knew it. "So then what happened?"

"Well." If Mama and Hulda hadn't been there, she wouldn't have gone on, but she had to. "Well, I just had to go to the bathroom, so I turned around to go back, and there was Uncle Hugh—"

"—coming from the little side hall into the main one," finished Greg triumphantly, "and there you were, as if you'd just come in from outside. So he never could have known or suspected you'd been upstairs. And he hadn't *seen* you go upstairs. But Mom and Aunt Alex saw you come out of the downstairs bathroom. So that's it, ladies. And I'll bet the whole thing didn't take more than about five minutes, which must have seemed less to you, Mom, out there on the front porch talking to Aunt Alex and Hulda, because you weren't paying any attention to time."

"That's right," said Mama. "And when Aunt Alex and I went back in while Uncle Hugh was getting in the car, and there was Julia coming out of the bathroom, we had no way of suspecting she'd already been upstairs." Mama sat there studying Julia, and Julia looked back at her. "Oh, such a mix-up because of you," she said. "And not saying anything is as good as telling a lie, Julia—you know that. Well, there's only one thing to do—and that's try to get in touch with Uncle Hugh. But, *how,* this being Saturday and his bank closed? And I haven't an idea where he's staying if he's with friends."

"Mama?" said Julia. "You know where he used to

live before he married Aunt Alex? I thought I wasn't supposed to tell that either, but we ought to tell him about Hulda and me. Shouldn't we?"

"Yes, Julia, we most certainly should."

"Well, after we were at the beach, Uncle Hugh and me, he took me up to that big gray house where he used to live—"

"Yes, the hotel," said Mama. "I remember—"

"And a man was just going to leave Uncle Hugh's room because he was getting married, and Uncle Hugh took me up there. Do you suppose—?"

"I'll bet anything!" exclaimed Mama. "Julia, do you want to tell Uncle Hugh about Aunt Alex's bottle if he's there, or shall I tell him? Oh, and there's my poor old kettle crackling and banging away to itself—"

Mama went out to the kitchen to make her tea and Julia looked at Hulda, then at Greg. And Greg stared at her.

"I'd never let anybody else tell what I'd done," he said. "I'd do my own telling."

"Oh, you're so perfect," said Mama, coming back in with her cup, but she was teasing, and she ruffled up his hair as she passed him.

"Well, I *wouldn't.*" And the bad part was, Julia knew he wouldn't.

She got up. "I'll tell him," she said. After all, it was Uncle Hugh. And he wasn't the person she dreaded. The very worst was to be left to the very last.

But as it turned out, after Mama had gotten the hotel and talked to the desk clerk, though Uncle Hugh was indeed staying there, he wasn't in and had left word for callers to give their names and phone numbers and he'd call them later. Of course the desk clerk didn't know when "later" would be.

"Well," said Mama, "that leaves everything still hanging. But, Hulda, won't you stay for dinner?"

Hulda couldn't. She must get home, she said, because Mrs. Anna would be waiting supper for both of them. "But you will call me, Julia? After you've talked to your Uncle Hugh?"

"Oh, Hulda"—and Julia flung her arms around Hulda—"of course I'll call you. Daddy wanted to, when he thought he was going to take me to Mrs. Anna's, but we didn't know her last name."

"Why, Rosenquist. Here, I'll write down the phone number, and you put it in your private telephone book. And now, goodbye, everybody. Goodness, it's almost six. Soon Mr. Redfern will be home expecting his dinner—"

After she'd gone, Mama went into the kitchen without a word to anyone and made herself another cup of tea because the first had gotten cold, and sat down at the kitchen table. And when Julia and Greg went out, there she was with her face in her hands, and her cup sitting there, untouched, with the steam rising from it.

"Mama?" said Julia.

"Just go away, you two," said Mama, not lifting her head. "Just go away and leave me alone. I want to be by myself—"

"Oh, *Mama*—" Julia dropped into her chair opposite, where she always sat. She couldn't bear being shut out—it was the worst feeling in the world, worse, even, than knowing she still had to face Aunt Alex.

Then, to Julia's astonishment, and surely to Greg's, too, because he came and sank down in his chair on the other side, Mama shoved back her cup of tea and put her head down on her folded arms on the table. And though they couldn't hear a sound from her, somehow Julia knew she was crying. And when she finally lifted her head after a long, wretched silence, Julia could see the tears and that her eyes were red.

"This is ridiculous!" she exclaimed angrily, "and I'm ashamed of myself. But I've had just about enough, that's all. I was dead tired when I got back from hunting—and everything is so ugly, and they want so much for their dark old apartments and dreadful, rackety little houses with either not a blade of grass or an old run-to-seed garden full of weeds. And I love this place. I thought when I got home how cool and peaceful and lovely it is—and the garden and everything, after Daddy and I have fixed it just the way we want it. And no sooner had I gotten in and slipped off my shoes and was going to have a cup of tea all to myself, than here came Maisie and Mrs. Woollard at

the front door, full of their news about how Julia had
gone away in her best clothes and gotten on the Dinky,
and Mr. Redfern had gone off *that* way, furious about
something, Maisie said, though her mother tried to
hush her.

"And was there anything Mrs. Woollard could do to
help? Poor dear, she said to me, it must be *so* exhaust-
ing to hunt for a new place, and then not to have Mr.
Redfern here—and where could Julia have got to?
Why would she go off in her best clothes, *by* herself,
and get on the Dinky? At *her* age! And no sooner had
Mrs. Woollard and that everlasting Maisie left, than
here was Grandma overflowing with helpful advice,
and oh, the humiliation of having Hulda hear our
private business. Never was I so ashamed—" Mama's
voice shook on the last word and Julia thought she was
going to cry again, but she didn't.

"And when I think of all the packing up to do—and
how we're to pay Aunt Alex for that bottle—*or* replace
it, I do not know. But you can't replace an heirloom,
and what she'll say when she knows how it happened,
I can't imagine, after her whole household being completely upset. And now here it is, six o'clock, or nearly,
and your father still not home. Where could he be?
And why would he stay away like this! Really, I don't
care a twit about getting dinner ready. Mr. Redfern
will be home and expecting his dinner, indeed! Well,
I'll tell you something. He can just expect. And you

can all of you get your dinner for yourselves—I'm
going to bed." And Mama got up from the table and
was going out of the kitchen, when Greg said,

"*I* know, Mom—let's go and meet him. He'll be
coming across the fields—"

"Oh, yes," said Julia, filled with sudden excitement,
"he *will* be. He's gone down to the wharf before to get
shrimps out of those big barrels. And maybe he'll be
starting back, or be partway across by now, where the
cows are. Remember?"

Mama turned and looked at them. And then, after
a moment or so, "Yes," she said under her breath,
"yes, so he will be, the wicked man. All right, then,
let's go."

11

The Evening Fields

Patchy wanted to come, too. No sooner were they outside and about to open the gate, than a black shape with white patches, tail high, came leaping along the path from the berry garden, beginning to be dusky now with the sun low over beyond San Francisco. As they opened the gate, he slipped out with them and looked up and said "Mya-a-a-a?" And kneaded his paws on the sidewalk, eagerly lifting one front foot and then the other as if he knew there was an evening walk in the offing, something he dearly loved.

"Oh, Patchy-cat," said Mama, "are you going to come with us? All that way?"

"Mrrff," said Patchy, and ran on ahead, his feet making a small, quick pattering, galloping, galloping, and he hid behind a tree. And when they came to him, out he pounced, tail twitching with excitement, head tossing coyly from side to side as if he'd done something frightfully clever, then off he went again until they couldn't see him. But when they turned left at the top of the rise to go along the field path that led to the wharves and the bay, here he came, rippling after them.

"Patchy, Patchy!" Julia swept him up. "I love you, Patchy-cat!" But he had other business to take care of now that they'd come to the fields, and he struggled to be let down. All they could detect, just barely in the fading light as they started along the path, was the quivering of the wild oats where he'd taken off after something that smelled delicious.

And now, there was the moon. It had been floating high, though faintly, but with the sun gone and the deep pink sunset glow that had flooded the vast fields faded as well, it cast a gossamer light. And a single star came out in the powerful evening blue: pure, brilliant, steady.

"But not a star, Jule," said Greg, when she called it that. "It's a planet, like ours. That's Venus. Planets reflect light. Suns are the real stars, and they don't reflect. They make their own light like our sun does."

"Oh," said Julia, silenced, and contented herself with watching Venus, watching its pale gold brightness, such a clear, pure brightness as she could hardly believe. Then as darkness came on, the moon's light deepened and washed like a ghostly tide over the fields. And there were the cows, a huddle of dark shapes off there just to the right of the path. Greg didn't seem to mind them, one way or the other, but Julia always moved in close to Daddy and took his hand when they came here on their walks. Now she moved in close to Mama, thinking they'd have to watch for the cowpats that sometimes landed on the path and that you had to be sure to step over com-*plete*-ly. Otherwise Mama got into a state about the smell in the house, and about your shoes, and all but made you clean them yourself.

"But what are the poor beasts doing out this time of night!" cried Mama. "Don't they need to be milked, Greg? Why aren't they bawling in agony? Why aren't they wending their way slowly o'er the lea, nose to tail, back to the barn?"

Greg didn't know, strangely enough, volume of reference that he usually was. It was a mystery, this herd of cows, out so late. But Greg went toward them, shooing them home. "Go on, now," he ordered in a loud, stern voice, "go on, go on," and waved his arms at them, running first to one side, then the other.

Amazingly, those that were standing rolled up the whites of their eyes at him, swung their heavy heads around and turned, and the lying-down ones heaved themselves up and they all went gallumphing away like heavy old boats in rough water, breasting great waves, their udders swaying. Then, nose to tail, they *did* wend slowly o'er the lea, apparently making for their barn.

"Why, *Greg,*" laughed Mama, "you should be a farmer. Those ab*surd* animals!"

Absurd animals, repeated Julia to herself with satisfaction. She liked that. She'd keep that—ab*surd* animals.

It was then she saw Daddy. She didn't exactly see him whole, but she knew he was there because she got the feeling of a very small dark object moving closer in the moonlight. "Daddy—Daddy—" she shrieked, and went racing toward him with Greg after her and then passing her, and it *was* Daddy, and when he held out both arms, Julia saw that he had a paper bag in each hand. But all the same he grabbed up his children, one under each arm, and hugged them.

And when Mama came to him, he let them drop, and he and Mama put their arms around each other and stood for several seconds without saying anything. Then he picked her up, right off the ground, and gave her a good, long, *firm* kiss before he put her down again. And Julia was hopping with excitement, just like Maisie. "You're a wicked man, Daddy—Mama said so. She said we'll go and meet him, the wicked man—"

Daddy laughed. "So I am—so I am! I'm sorry, Celia. I've been a bad, wicked fellow, but I'll tell you why.

You see, I started off, thinking and thinking, and didn't know what time it was or where I was going, but of course I set off in the same old direction, and I don't even remember going down toward the fields, or crossing them. And when I looked up, I couldn't believe it. There were the wharves, not the first lot, but the second, much farther along, and I could see by the sun that I wouldn't get back until after dark, but I thought it was silly to be down there and not buy shrimps and watercress and that good bread they make at the little bakery, and some lemon and raspberry boats and lemon curd, so I did. It only took me ten minutes, but all the same I was feeling guilty, so I phoned home and you weren't there—"

"Already started off," said Greg.

Oh, *boy,* thought Julia. Lemon and raspberry boats and lemon curd. The boats were little rich, biscuity shapes like rowboats filled with raspberry jam or with lemon jam, called curd. And you could buy the curd separately, if you wanted, and spread it on your toast for breakfast.

Now Julia, unable to keep her news back any longer, told Daddy all about going off without him on the Dinky to Mrs. Anna's because she wanted to surprise him, and how she'd told Mrs. Anna and Hulda what she'd done at Aunt Alex's, and everything that had happened about the boys knocking her down, and then Hulda bringing her home. Daddy groaned at the idea of his going off and leaving her to do such a crazy thing, and said "Great Scott!" when she told him about getting lost and the boys knocking her over and stealing her money.

"Blast and thunderation!" he exclaimed. "I can't turn my back for a second—"

"Indeed you can't," said Mama, "and I hope you remember that. I told you you were a wicked man, knowing Julia as you do. And what's more, I *didn't* find a place for us—they're all as ugly as sin, or far too expensive, or too small, or run-down, and Mrs. Woollard and Maisie came over, knowing all there is to be knowed—"

"Like Toad," said Greg.

"Yes, like Toad—about us and our private doings, and Grandma came over and advised me how to run my life, and it was just awful. And I think it's heavenly out here in the fields and I'd like to stay out here forever, and never, *never* go back—!"

Then they were all quiet, Greg on one side of Daddy, Mama on the other, and Julia trotting on ahead, beginning to feel very wavery and peculiar. And the next thing she knew she was up on Daddy's back with her arms around his neck, her head resting against his, and her legs held firm in his arms. And Mama and Daddy and Greg were singing together in harmony (Daddy very low the way he always did, and Mama and Greg higher),

Eggs and bacon for my break-fast,
A nice lump of mutton for my tea,
A shoulder of lamb for my dinner
  and my lunch—
Be gentle and kind to me-e-e—
Plenty of toast for my su-upper,
Then off to bed we'll crawl,
And we'll cling together
  like the i-ivy
On the old ga-ar-den wall—

Julia chuckled in her delicious drowsiness and tried to join in, but all she could manage was a soft sort of buzzing. Then she fell fast asleep again and when she came awake they were going in at their own gate and along the walk. She looked down and there was Patchy, bouncing along beside them, letting out short, eager cries that said as plain as plain could be that he knew his dinner was about to appear before him at last, most any moment.

"Patchy!" she said. "You're an ab-*surd* animal—"

Mama laughed, running up the steps. "Now where do you suppose she got that expression?"

Much, much later, at least so Julia felt, because everything was dark, she was awakened by horrible goings-on right outside her French doors. She was in bed, all tucked up. And Patchy-cat and his fierce rival, the tough old tom that Daddy called Mordred, or Mordy for short, were singing songs of loathing at each other. Up they went, and down, tenor and bass, a long drawn-out, acid chorus that said, "Don't move, or I'll claw your eyes out—" and "You wouldn't dare— You touch me and I'll rip your throat—" and then the terrifying interruptions of spitting and screaming matches in which it seemed that both Patchy and Mordy must surely be torn to bloody shreds. Then the low, bitter yowlings again, until there was a furious rattling at the front door.

"Patchy—get out of there!" And Daddy charged around the side of the front porch toward Julia's room and there was a frantic scrabbling in the bushes as Mordy no doubt escaped, with Patchy close behind him, right at the tip of his old crooked, bitten tail. *"Get* in here, you rascally cat—" But whether Patchy obeyed and came in, Julia couldn't make out. Probably not, because at this moment he was no longer a loving family member, but a ferocious beast of the jungle with no human connections whatever.

"Sister," whispered Julia after a little, for something had been nipping at her in her sleep, "Sister, I did *so* think the little animal on the top of the perfume bottle was magic, didn't I? And I did *so* think it came together and was all mended and whole, didn't I?"

But strangely enough, Sister was silent. Julia waited, and still Sister didn't say a single word. And so finally Julia fell asleep again, picturing herself, perhaps as early as tomorrow, standing before Aunt Alex.

12

———————

The Queen on
the Stairs

Mama was talking on the phone when Julia came out in her pajamas the next morning, Sunday, to see what was going on. She had lemon and raspberry boats in mind, and lemon curd, and was about to demand indignantly if everybody had eaten hers at dinner last night. Because she hadn't had her dinner! This dawned on her at just the moment she woke up. *No dinner.* But she couldn't accuse anybody of the theft of her lemon and raspberry boats, because Daddy was splashing in the bathroom, Greg was off and away (there were sounds of him and Bob next door in Bob's backyard) and Mama was on the phone talking to Uncle Hugh.

"Yes, Hugh," she said, turning a little as Julia came into the kitchen, "I know, but of course as long as

we're bringing Hulda over with us—" Silence, while
Uncle Hugh said something. Then Mama again,
"Well, I'm not going to tell you myself what it's all
about, but here's somebody who wants to have a word
with you." Mama studied Julia gravely as she handed
her the receiver. Julia put her suddenly cold paws
behind her back, but at that instant she remembered
Greg. "I'd never let anybody else tell what I'd done.
I'd do my own telling." She swallowed and took the
receiver and went close to the phone.

"Hello, Uncle Hugh."

"Well, Julia, you little monkey," he said. "What's all
this you people are up to? So you told where I am!"

Silence, while Julia swallowed again. "I had to tell,
Uncle Hugh. Or at least I only said you took me up
there—because I got to thinking about where you
might be, and Mama said oh, she bet anything!"

"Ah, yes," said Uncle Hugh, "so that was it. Where
else would I go but to my old hotel! But, Julia, what's
all this about bringing Hulda over?" Another silence,
while Julia's heart was pumping away uncommonly
fast.

"Well, you see," she began, "Hulda didn't do anything. And she's got to go back to your house. She's
got to, and so I went to see her to tell—"

"*You* went to see her!"

"Yes, by myself, because Daddy went off, but he
said before he left that I had to tell Hulda. And so
I—"

"Had to tell Hulda what, Julia?"

"About what I—" And here her voice began fading out the way it always did when she got to this part. "About the little bottle—"

Silence, now, on Uncle Hugh's end of the line, while Julia waited, her heart thudding. "Oh, I *see,*" he said at last. "I understand, even though I can't imagine just when you managed it. But it doesn't matter—we won't go into it now, and of course you must all come over and bring Hulda and I'll phone Aunt Alex and get her to come home, and we will all meet. And just speak right up, Julia. Say your piece and tell Aunt Alex how you feel about what you've done. The best thing is to just plunge in. Aunt Alex will be so relieved about Hulda, I can tell you. You can't imagine how relieved she'll be!" Here Uncle Hugh actually let out a little laugh.

"The thing is," said Julia, "you'll never trust me again, will you?"

"Don't be a silly," he answered. "Of course I will. Just you try me. And now let me talk to your mother and we'll get everything settled about the time. And you keep your chin up."

Well, it was strange. Julia thought it would be the most awful business she'd ever have to go through— to climb those cement steps between the two big lions lying on either side of the entrance to Aunt Alex and Uncle Hugh's front walk. And then there were the

steps up to the front porch, and then you had to wait
while somebody came to the door. Julia thought for
sure, while she stood at the railing of the ferry watching in blackest gloom as the docks of San Francisco
came nearer and nearer, that she'd probably be sick
and vomit. She sometimes did that when she got too
worked up.

But here she was, going up those cement steps, and
then up the steps to the porch, and then waiting for
that immensely tall, heavy front door to open. (It was
painted a darkish green with a huge golden knocker on
it, which Greg said wasn't gold at all, but polished
brass, though all the same Julia went right on saying
"golden" to herself.) And she didn't feel a bit sick.
Only tight and tingling all over. She couldn't wait to
tell Aunt Alex the truth!

And the reason was this: She also couldn't wait to
see Aunt Alex turn to Hulda, hold out both hands, and
say, "Oh, Hulda—I'm so sorry! And to think I thought
you were to blame. Will you forgive me?"

Julia knew all about that. Daddy often held out his
hands to Mama after he'd been wicked and gone off
inside himself and not said anything for the longest
time, being in a mood, or going off alone for a walk
and not telling anybody, like yesterday. She knew all
about people apologizing and saying they were sorry.
But she'd never once seen Aunt Alex say this to Uncle
Hugh, or to anybody. But now Aunt Alex would have
to say it to Hulda. There was no way out.

Would it be Aunt Alex who opened the door? No, it was Uncle Hugh. And he looked at them all and smiled, then swooped up Julia when she went to him just the way she swooped up Patchy-cat, and gave her a big hug and kiss. Then he kissed everybody else, including Hulda—but not Daddy, of course!—because he was so happy. Then he led them in, and there was Aunt Alex, moving majestically down the curving staircase, the kind Julia was sure they had in castles. Because she always saw this house, this hallway with its shining floor and beautiful rug and enormous mirror over the table filled with flowers, as the place where fairy tales happened inside castles. And Aunt Alex was coming down these stairs just now as if she were a queen looking down over her subjects.

She paused halfway and took them all in, her eyes resting longest on Hulda. One hand lay lightly on the banister and the other played with the string of pearls around her neck.

"Well, Hulda," she said, her expression never changing, her voice cool, though she sounded a little surprised, "so here you are." She came down slowly a step or two farther. "Now what's all this about, everybody? Hugh phoned me and said I had to come home and that he would come and get me. I thought there must be some crisis."

Eagerly Julia ran forward and stood at the bottom of the stairs. "Aunt Alex, it's because I have something to tell you. Hulda didn't do anything—she absolutely

didn't. It was me. I went up to your bedroom and picked up your bottle and it dropped, and the little animal broke in two, and I didn't say anything because I thought—" But here Julia had to stop, to her own immense surprise. Because she had, of course, been going to tell Aunt Alex how she'd thought the little animal was magic and had mended itself. But she couldn't. "Because I—because I thought—" and then there were no more words to go on.

Aunt Alex did not reply at once.

"Well," she said after a silence in which Julia had grown hotter and hotter, but could only stand there at the foot of the stairs, looking up, waiting for Aunt Alex to say something. "So it was you, Julia. I might have known, only that I can't understand when you could have done it. But you are a very, *very* naughty girl— it was really quite unforgivable to say nothing about it." She put her hand to her forehead and closed her eyes as if she were getting another of her headaches again. And so she was. "My head is pounding—and now, this! My whole house upset because of you—"

"I'm sorry, Aunt Alex, I'm sorry—but Hulda's *here.* She's come back—aren't you even going to—?"

Aunt Alex took her hand down and gazed out over Julia's head, over Uncle Hugh's and Mama's and Daddy's and Greg's, to where Hulda was still standing near the door with her suitcase beside her.

"Naturally," she said, "I'm much relieved that this

house can settle down again and we can all go on from where we left off. Please do accept, Hulda, that I'm pleased you've returned after going away with scarcely a word. And now, if you'll forgive me, one and all, I really must go back to my room—" And she turned and started up.

"But, Aunt Alex!" Julia couldn't believe it—she felt bitterly cheated. "Aren't you going to tell Hulda you're sorry—thinking it was her? Because she wasn't to blame—she didn't *do*—"

"Julia!" said Mama sharply. "That's enough. Alex, I want you to know that Julia and I are going to replace your bottle. We'll go to the antique shops and try to find something for you, even though I know we can't really replace what you've lost. After all, something you felt was priceless, a museum piece and an heirloom—"

Aunt Alex gazed down at Mama with a slight frown between her brows. "What on earth do you mean, Celia? What's all this about a museum?"

"But that's what you said, Mrs. Alex," came Hulda's voice, level, and as cool as Aunt Alex's had been. "That's what made me feel especially bad. Don't you remember when you found the bottle broken and called me upstairs, how you told me it was a museum piece and an heirloom, because it was handed down from your great-grandmother, and that it was priceless?"

"Oh, good heavens!" cried Aunt Alex, "did I really? Well, of course, I was appalled, because it had been perfect in the morning. And it *was* a treasure— at least I'm sure my mother gave it to me. But as for being a museum piece and priceless, you know how it is when you're upset. And of course I *was*—frightfully upset, to think that no one would have said anything. But now I must go upstairs—my head is absolutely throbbing. Please go in, everybody, and, Hulda, when do you suppose you could serve dinner?" Aunt Alex paused for a moment in her regal movement upward.

"Around three, I think, Mrs. Alex."

"Good! Very well, then, you may expect me down at three—" And Aunt Alex continued her ascent and disappeared along the upper hallway.

13

These Grown-Ups!

"Well, I'll be confounded," said Daddy under his breath, so low that no doubt only Julia, standing nearby, heard him.

Uncle Hugh turned and went to Hulda and picked up her bag. "Hulda," he said, "I apologize for all that's happened. You will stay, won't you?"

Hulda looked up at him, her little thin face bleak under the blonde hair brushed straight back into a knot, her bright blue eyes searching his as if to find an answer she wasn't sure of. Then she looked away.

"I don't know, Mr. Hugh," she said in a flat voice. "I thought at first, after Julia told me what she'd done and that she'd tell her Aunt Alex, that everything would be all right. But now—no, I'm not at all certain. We shall have to see."

"Hulda," said Mama, "I have a feeling everything's going to settle down. I know it will—I *know* it. And now, let Julia and Greg and me help you—"

"Oh, no, Mrs. Redfern, I couldn't have that—at least, maybe the children could help, because I'm going to have to hustle. Mr. Hugh did my shopping for me on his way to pick up Mrs. Alex—"

"Well, I can at least get out the big tablecloth," said Mama. "That's something the children and I can do, set the table. But they couldn't manage that tablecloth alone—they'd get it all wrinkled."

So the hustle began, and Mama and Greg flung the long, thick, rich linen tablecloth across the dining room table, and Mama smoothed it all over and put a vase of flowers in the center. Then Julia put around the silver just exactly as she was told to, and Greg brought in the goblets and put one at each place. Then Hulda set Julia and Greg to shelling the peas and sent Mama away. But when they were finished, it seemed as if she couldn't take their chatter any longer. She had to be alone, she said.

"I'm not myself, children, that's the truth of it. I've got to think—and if I'm to have dinner ready on time, I can't have any distractions anyway, so you two run along."

Gloomily, Julia went off with Greg to Uncle Hugh's study. "Greg?" she said when they were hunched up on Uncle Hugh's leather couch, one in each corner with their arms around their knees. "*Why* wouldn't

Aunt Alex come down and say she was sorry to
Hulda?''

"Well, because she *couldn't*." And Greg sounded as
if Julia should have known this. "She just couldn't, not
in front of everybody. She's got to be on top." Yes.
Julia saw Aunt Alex, halfway up the stairs, looking
down across the rest of them. "And she couldn't have
been on top if she'd had to apologize. But the thing is,
it might turn out she never will. And if she doesn't,
things'll never be right with Hulda and Aunt Alex.
And Hulda'll leave again, and it'll be all your fault."
He stared coldly at her.

She looked down to escape his eyes and wanted to
cry in the worst way, but somehow she couldn't. She
just felt sick at her stomach.

"I hate Aunt Alex."

"Well, that's a fine thing! After all, you were the one
who busted her bottle. *You* began it all. Why in heck
didn't you tell Mom and Dad?" Then he thought for
a moment. "But you'd still have had to tell Aunt Alex.
Though at least if you had, she wouldn't have blamed
Hulda. That's the worst part—Hulda being blamed.
So Aunt Alex can't back down now and admit she was
wrong. She's got to save her dignity."

"What's that mean—'save her diginty'? What's 'diginty'?"

"*Not* diginty, Jule. '*Dig*-nity.' It means her pride.
She's awfully stiff in the neck about always being on

top of everything. I'll bet it really got her when Hulda left. I'll bet if Hulda had stuck around, creeping up and down stairs apologetically like a little kid who's been scolded, Aunt Alex would kindly have forgiven her after a week or two. But Hulda wouldn't do that. She didn't break the bottle, and if she had, she'd have told. So she went. Good for Hulda."

Yes, thought Julia fiercely, *good for Hulda!*

"Boy, just think," Greg went on, "that bottle wasn't priceless and a museum piece after all."

At three o'clock sharp, Hulda, with pink cheeks and two or three strands of hair escaping their knot, announced to Uncle Hugh and the rest of them that dinner was about to be served. So Uncle Hugh went up to tell Aunt Alex.

But the minute Aunt Alex came into the dining room, Julia felt her stomach get all "intertwangled"— her own private word that meant it felt tight and squirmish. "Not 'squirmish,' Jule," Greg had told her more than once. "You mean 'squeamish.' " "No, I do not mean 'squeamish,' " Julia would say. "My stomach feels all squirmy and I mean 'squirmish.' "

The Redferns were waiting at their places, and Uncle Hugh drew out Aunt Alex's chair at one end of the table and then went to his own place at the other.

The trouble was that Aunt Alex didn't seem a bit changed from the way she had been on the stairs. She had on a different dress now and looked more beautiful than ever. But her face was expressionless, and she sat there with one hand in her lap and the other turning and turning a little crystal dish near her. She seemed a very, very long way away from them, not making the least effort to be friendly or to answer Uncle Hugh's cheery little remarks while they ate their salads.

Now Hulda came in with a huge platter of fried chicken and set it down in front of Uncle Hugh, and Greg brought in a bowl of green beans in one hand and a bowl of what Julia knew was spoon bread in the other. This was her utmost favorite thing to go with fried chicken—all fluffy and soft, it was, made out of eggs and cornmeal and milk, with a crusty golden top on it.

Now at last Aunt Alex lifted her eyes and followed Hulda in what she was doing. And it seemed to Julia as if something was filling up and up, like a glass being filled to the brim until it was almost spilling over because everything was so uncomfortable and getting more so. Somehow, not even Daddy or Greg could answer Uncle Hugh's remarks the way they usually did. He looked at Julia once and sent her a little wink, and she sent him back a smile, not because she felt like it but because she didn't want to fail him.

And then even he was quiet and the only sounds left were their knives and forks on their plates, very loud, going *clink, clink*. Then Hulda brought in biscuits—

hot, fragrant, golden brown biscuits, and Uncle Hugh stopped eating to gaze up at her.

"I don't see," he said, "how on earth you did it all, Hulda. How could you possibly? In the time you had?"

Mama said something, and so did Daddy, quick, both at once, and Greg and Julia—how good everything was and how the spoon bread had turned out exactly right. Hulda stopped behind Julia's chair, one small red hand resting on Julia's head. "Oh, I can usually do what I want to do, Mr. Hugh, if I'm determined enough."

Then she went out again and came back with two bowls of her jam, apricot and plum, and put one at Uncle Hugh's end and one at Aunt Alex's. As she reached to set it in front of Aunt Alex, an amazing thing happened.

All at once Aunt Alex's hand came out and she caught Hulda by the arm. "Oh, Hulda, Hulda—!" she cried in the oddest, most stifled voice Julia had ever heard from her. And her other hand went to her mouth and she sat there for a second as if she didn't know what to do with herself. Then in a sudden, quick movement she pushed her chair back and got up and, with an arm around Hulda's shoulders, went with her toward the butler's pantry. Julia, in her place next to Daddy on her chair with two cushions on it, watched for an instant then slipped down.

But, no. Something stopped her. That was private,

what Aunt Alex and Hulda would have to say to each other. She'd be exactly like Maisie, always wanting to butt in on things that were none of her business. So she got back onto her chair and everybody began talking and laughing and being happy the way they usually were at this table. The glass had brimmed over.

But in the living room afterwards, when Greg had had his chance to tell Uncle Hugh and Aunt Alex and Daddy just precisely the way it worked out that nobody had suspected Julia of being the one who'd broken the bottle top and cracked the bottle, she had a question to ask.

"Didn't any of you ever do anything *awful* when you were kids? Were all of you just perfect?"

"*Per*fect!" exclaimed Aunt Alex, and one dark, silky eyebrow went up. "I'll never forget—" and she stopped.

"*What?*" shouted Julia. "*What,* Aunt Alex?"

"Cutting all the bugle beads off my mother's best Paris dress."

Everybody drew a breath of horror. No!

"*Yes,*" said Aunt Alex. "I was thirteen and my parents were still treating me as if I were a mere child, wouldn't let me do anything or go anywhere. Or so I thought and so I told them. And when I got furious one day and answered my mother back, she took me upstairs and locked me in a closet. Unfortunately, it was where her good dresses were hanging, and there were various sewing things in there, kept in boxes on the shelf, including a pair of scissors. So I just cut all the bugle beads off Mother's most beautiful dress, all around the hem, then climbed out of the window into the rain, shinnied down the drainpipe, and ran away to my best friend's."

Aunt Alex *shinnied*?

Everyone gazed at her in absolute astonishment, and she gazed right back at them like an actress who has just come out onto the stage after a dramatic final curtain. Julia, her eyes wide and her mouth open, was trying to imagine Aunt Alex—large, heavy Aunt Alex, with her big bosom that beads hung over as if over a cliff—shinnying down a drainpipe.

"Oh, Alex!" cried Mama. "What did your mother do?"

Aunt Alex gave a little chuckle. "Do? I'll tell you what she did. When she finally got me back, my father gave me one of the spankings of my life, and Mother made me sew every one of those blasted bugle beads back around the hem. And I had to do it just so. I'd a million times rather have had another licking than that—it was ghastly. And it took me three solid weeks."

Julia, who had her arms around her knees as usual, put her head back, rocked around on her footstool, and laughed and laughed, and so did everyone else.

What a story! Oh, these grown-ups! But to cut off all those beads, thought Julia. She could never do that to Mama. No, not to Mama. She loved her too much.

14

Another Surprise

A tall, rather nice-looking older man was standing outside the Redferns' gate when Mrs. Woollard called over and said that the Redferns were out. Could she be of any help? Could she take a message or anything? Well, the man said, could she tell him when the Redferns might be back? She came over very fast and said she wasn't sure, but she'd be more than happy to take a message.

Julia, out in the berry garden with Patchy and Sister, this late Saturday afternoon a week after the goings-on at Aunt Alex and Uncle Hugh's, heard all this. Greg was over at Bob's house as usual, and Julia had been with Maisie on her front porch playing Parcheesi when Mama left for the grocery store and called to Julia that she'd be right back. But Julia and Maisie had quarreled, so Maisie went up to her room and Julia came on home. Mrs. Woollard didn't know about all this because she'd been in her kitchen, then gone out front to water the lawn.

Julia came from the berry garden and looked at the tall man with the lined brown face and kind eyes. And he looked at her and smiled.

"Why, Julia Redfern," cried Mrs. Woollard, "I thought you were up in her room with Maisie."

"No," said Julia. "She cheats."

"Well," said Mrs. Woollard, drawing in her mouth, "I expect she isn't the only one. This gentleman would like to see your parents, so I think it would be best if he came back later."

"No, Mama'll be right here. She's just gone to the grocery store. She said she'd be back in fifteen minutes."

"Oh," said Mrs. Woollard. "I see," and rather looked the tall gentleman up and down out of the sides of her eyes while trying not to let it show she was.

"I'm Eugene Tattersall," he said, as if knowing what Mrs. Woollard was doing. "I've bought this house from Mrs. Weed, so of course I wanted a little visit with the Redferns. I'll stay right out here in the garden and talk to Julia, and if you're concerned about me, here's my card and you could call Mrs. Weed to be sure I'm who I say I am—"

"Oh, Mr. Tattersall," laughed Mrs. Woollard in a

high, ladylike voice, "oh, that's perfectly all right. I just had to be sure—"

"Of course you did, Madam. I don't blame you in the least. And now, thank you very much. Julia and I will have our little talk."

Mrs. Woollard looked at Julia, then at Mr. Tattersall, murmured a few little polite remarks, and went back to her watering, but did not fail to give a good stare across every now and then.

"Come in, Mr. Tattersall," said Julia. And she opened the gate. "Would you like to sit in the gardening chair?" *Garden* chair, Greg would tell her. The chair didn't do any gardening, and Mama didn't garden while she sat in it. But Julia didn't see what all that had to do with anything, so she went right on calling it a gardening chair.

"Why, yes, Julia, thank you—that's very kind," said Mr. Tattersall. "But where will you sit?"

"Oh, on the grass here. Would you like a cup of tea?"

"A cup of tea?" exclaimed Mr. Tattersall, lowering himself into the chair and slinging one extremely long leg over the other. "Why, could you make me a cup of tea?"

"Well, I don't know. But I could try. Mama always says that to company. 'Shall I make you a cup of tea?' "

"Julia, do you know, I don't think I could manage one."

"Well, would you like an apple? I would."

"All right. I think I would like an apple—very much."

"Be right back," said Julia, and she went into the kitchen, got two big red apples, crisp and sweet and juicy, as she well knew, washed them off as Mama had shown her how to do, standing on a stool at the sink, and took them out, all wet, to Mr. Tattersall. He got out his handkerchief, dried his off, and took a big bite.

"Oh, my!" he said. "What an apple!" He chewed. Then, "Well, now, Julia, I've come to get acquainted with you and your mother and father—"

"And Greg," said Julia. "He's my brother. He's eight and I'm six."

"Why, yes, of course—Greg. Though I don't remember Mrs. Weed mentioning Greg so much. She seemed only to talk about you."

"She doesn't like me, does she? She told me once not to play under the house because I'd get dirty. But me and Maisie don't get dirty under there, and neither does Brucie Clemens. We just play doctor and he gets operated on and yells and groans and we have a lot of fun. But Mrs. Weed came and saw us and got awfully mad and I wanted to tell her we weren't getting dirty, but she came to see Mama. She said she wanted to sell the house. And Mama said, but Daddy painted everything and they cleaned the bricks. But we have to go anyway."

"Your father did the painting and cleaning?" said Mr. Tattersall, looking quite surprised.

"Yes. Didn't Mrs. Weed tell you?"

"Well, no—I thought she said that—but what's all this about you having to go away? Why are you going?"

Julia stared at him. "But Mrs. Weed *said* we have to. Because it's your house now. She said we have to get another place, and so Mama's been hunting and hunting—"

"Well, I'll be con-founded," muttered Mr. Tattersall to himself, just exactly the way Daddy did after Aunt Alex had gone back up the winding stairs like a queen and said she'd be down at three sharp.

Now here came Mama along the street, the upper part of her with her bag of groceries showing above the fence. When she saw Julia and Mr. Tattersall, she stopped in surprise, then came along to the gate and was about to open it when Mr. Tattersall sprang up, hastened over, opened it for her, and took her bag of groceries after saying very politely, "May I?" And then, "Mrs. Redfern?" he asked.

"Why, yes—"

"I'm Eugene Tattersall, the new owner of your house, and Julia and I have been having quite a conversation. She was so good as to get me an apple— it was very refreshing."

"Mama?" said Julia, "Was that all right?"

Mama laughed. "I only hope you washed Mr. Tattersall's apple."

"Oh, she did—she did—and we've been sitting here

in the garden until you came back. We've been talking about Mrs. Weed."

"Ah!" said Mama, and she looked at him and at Julia with that merry twinkle she sometimes got in her eyes. "Well, I can only hope that Julia has been discreet— though, actually, I don't have much hope. Julia is rarely discreet. Please do come in, Mr. Tattersall. I'm happy to know you," and she held out her hand and he shook it and gave a little bow in spite of the bag of groceries.

They all went into the house, and Julia looked back at the very last second and there was Maisie peeking out from behind one of the posts of the Woollard front porch. Julia chuckled and closed the door behind her.

Mama made Mr. Tattersall a cup of coffee, which he said he preferred, and herself a cup of tea and came and sat down. *"Now,"* she said, "we can talk."

"Mrs. Redfern," said Mr. Tattersall, "I'm very much puzzled. I hear from Julia that you and your husband did all the painting and freshening up around here, when I understood from Mrs. Weed that—"

"Yes, I know," said Mama, with a little ironical smile. "That impression *was* given out. But we did it. Every inch of it. *And* paid for the paint and whatever else was needed."

"What is more," Mr. Tattersall went on, "I hear from Julia that you understand that you must move."

"Why, ye-es," said Mama, gazing at Mr. Tattersall

with the strangest expression, in which there was the smallest trace of hope. "Don't tell me that you—"

"Why, yes, I *do* tell you that you need not move. In fact, I told Mrs. Weed expressly that I like so much the way you people have kept the garden and taken care of the house, that I will be delighted to have you for tenants."

Mama carefully put down her cup and saucer on the little table at her end of the couch, leaned back, and laid a hand each side of her face, while Julia stared at Mr. Tattersall from Sister's chair.

"You mean we can *stay*?" she demanded of him.

"Why, of course."

Julia leaped up and clapped her hands together. "You see, Mama—you see?" she shouted. "I told you that Mrs. Weed is an old witch—I *told* you!"

Mama studied Mr. Tattersall for a moment. "You have no idea," she said then, "you can't possibly have any idea what this means to me, to hear you say that. I've been so unhappy hunting for something that would even begin to take the place of this house. You see, we love it here, which is why we were willing to put so much work into it. In fact, we hoped to buy it one of these days. But if we could stay for a while—"

"Well, of course, of course," exclaimed Mr. Tattersall. "That's what I had in mind. I won't be retiring for five years yet—and whether my wife and I will want to move here then, I don't know. But tell me when you're ready to buy, and we'll see how things stand, how my wife feels about it by then. How's that?"

Mama looked at Mr. Tattersall blissfully, then picked up her cup and took a little quick swallow. "Oh, I can't wait for my husband to get home. He's a writer —and you can't think how he dreaded getting all packed up!"

After that, Mama and Mr. Tattersall went on talking about things like the plumbing and the state of the shingles on the roof, so Julia went off to tell Sister and Patchy what had happened. Only Sister was in Julia's room, and after telling her the happy news, she went outside to find Patchy to let him know that he need not be shut in a closet, after all, while the moving men were here. "Poor Patchy," Mama had said the other night, "he'll be absolutely terrified. Yet the only thing to do would be to shut him in a closet while the house is emptied. And then he'll have to get used to a new place, but if we take an apartment, we may not be allowed to keep him."

Not keep Patchy? Julia couldn't believe this: that Mama and Daddy would allow such an outrageous thing to happen.

"Then we won't *go* into any old apartment!"

"We may have to, Julia. And there's no use raising your voice."

But now they *wouldn't* have to—they *wouldn't*. And Bob and Greg could go on being best friends, collecting their train and streetcar stuff, and Julia and Maisie could go on being—well, maybe not friends exactly, but at least they could go on playing together.

At a certain season of the year, the big old buckeye tree at the end of the garden let fall its buckeyes, smooth, round seeds as big as golf balls and covered with a satiny, reddish-brown skin, which Mama cut with a very sharp penknife into patterns. These she lifted off and there, underneath the curved and delicate shapes she had cut, would be revealed the ivory meat of the nut. What wondrous buckeyes she made —the ivory patterns gleaming out against the reddish-brown skin.

Julia went out to look at the buckeye tree and to find Patchy. And there he was, sitting at the side of the bucket Mama kept under the garden faucet, where the pipe stuck up at the side of the path leading to the berry garden. And when a drip fell, he would reach out a paw to try and catch it. Julia went over and knelt beside him and looked in. And there was Patchy's face and Julia's side by side. "Sweet water, clear water," thought Julia. "Badger's face, squirrel's, and hare's, mountain lion's, fox's, and great brown bear's." That was Daddy's poem, or almost. "Patchy," she said into his ear, very softly, "you don't have to be shut in a closet. And Mrs. Weed told a big fib. And we can stay forever—"

"Ah-ah-ah-ah," said Patchy, looking up at her. And the way he blinked, it seemed as if he were saying, "Ah-ah-ah, what a relief!"

A wave of the most intense happiness flowed over Julia. "Oh, Patchy, Patchy," and she gathered him up, and then Maisie came running across the street, so she let him slip away when Maisie pushed open the gate.

"What'd you find out, Julia?" shouted Maisie eagerly. "What'd you find out? When d'you have to go?"

Julia sat on the grass cross-legged and looked up at Maisie with a little smile. She waited for a moment or two, just to whet Maisie's curiosity.

"We don't *have* to go," she said finally. "Mr. Tattersall told Mama we can stay just as long as we like. And that Mrs. Weed *is* an old witch—"

Maisie gawked at her. "I don't believe it!" she burst out. "I don't believe it!" and her black eyes sparked with disappointment. A great big one-up for Julia.

Julia shrugged. "I don't care—*don't* believe it."

"Well, how come he's going to let you stay?" demanded Maisie. "Why doesn't *he* want to live here?"

Julia rolled over onto her back and bicycled for a second or two. To tell the truth, she wasn't sure about that herself. But she'd heard a big kid say something the other day, something she'd been saving especially for a moment like this. "That's for me to know and you to find out." Then she let her legs fall and studied that pale, furious face.

Maisie's chin went up and she was about to answer, when, "Mai-ai-sie!" came the call from the Woollards' front porch. "Time for din-ner—" And Mrs. Woollard stood there, waiting.

"I have to go," announced Maisie with dignity. "*I* always set the table for *my* mother."

"Well, so do I," said Julia.

"Oh, soda water," shot back Maisie, and turned and flashed out the gate and across the street and up the front steps. "Mama—Mama," she yelled, "guess what! That man who came—he told Mrs. Redfern they don't *have* to go—" and the door banged behind her and all was quiet.

15

The Little Room

"Oh, Harry," said Mama out in the hall after she'd tucked Julia in and drawn the door closed all but an inch. "Harry, I'm so happy, I can't believe it—"

Daddy began singing another of his silly songs.

> Then pretty Polly in the flat
> Cries out to the old tabby cat—
> "Kiss Mama, kiss Papa,
> And we'll all say—good night—"

and the light in the hall went out, and Mama and Daddy went off together to their own bedroom.

Julia had her arms around Patchy as she fell asleep, but now her arm was no longer around him. It was slipped through Hulda's, for she was sitting beside Hulda on the train in the little room with the narrow corridor outside. There they were, close together, Julia next to the window looking out at the passing countryside, the green meadows like parks, and the thick woods, and then the green meadows again, sweeping by, fast—fast. And when they'd go through a narrow, dug-out place that Hulda said was called a cutting, the *click-click, click-click* of the train wheels would have a different sound, so that Julia would have known with her eyes closed that they were going through a cutting. Now Hulda was saying that they must have lunch, because, look—everyone was getting down suitcases.

"But, Hulda, don't you remember? We don't have any lunch—I have to get out at the next station and buy some sandwiches and an orange apiece."

Hulda gave a little laugh, reached up and got down their suitcase and opened it. And Julia's eyes widened, for there were a whole lot of plates packed away in it.

"Please," said Hulda to everyone in the little room, "won't you share with us?" She began handing around the beautiful plates, dinner plates with flowers around the center in a border, and a gold rim around the edge. All the women let out cries of amazement and turned them over to see what kind they were, and then *ting*ed them with the first finger and thumb. That's the way you could tell if a plate was good, Mama said. The plate had to go *ting!*

Then Hulda handed around big linen napkins and got out an enormous platter of hot, golden fried chicken, so enormous that there was loads of chicken for everybody, and then a casserole of spoon bread with a big spoon stuck in the side. And everyone was so surprised they let out cries of excitement and eagerness. They took all they wanted, and there was plenty left on the platter and in the casserole.

Now Hulda handed them a bowl of gravy to go on the spoon bread, and next a big basket of hot, buttered biscuits, and after that a dish of fruit salad.

The men and women ate and ate and ate, gazing at each other with eyes of astonishment, and letting out moans of satisfaction every now and then. And Julia and Hulda ate, too, because by now Hulda had finished handing out and had clicked the suitcase closed and stood it up at her feet.

But next, the biggest surprise of all. When everybody had finished the chicken and spoon bread and fruit and biscuits, Hulda took up the suitcase again, opened it, and drew out a plate much, much larger than the dinner plates, with a big mound of something white and glossy on it. The smooth white glossy stuff was golden brown on all its little waves and swirls, and that was because, Hulda told Julia, she had baked it in the oven.

And when Hulda took out a silver sort of spade from the suitcase, and cut into the mound, Julia saw that there was pink ice cream inside sitting on white cake.

"But how can you *bake* ice cream, Hulda?" This was the strangest kind of cooking Julia had ever heard of.

"But that's what you do, Julia," said Hulda. "You put the ice cream on the cake, then you put the meringue all over it"—"merang" was the way Julia heard the word—"and then you pop it in a hot, hot oven for four or five minutes—and that's it."

Now everyone was handed a clean plate with a thick slice of dessert on it, and there were more moans of delight and satisfaction. Then at last everyone thanked Hulda, and she folded up the napkins, took all the plates, packed them away in the suitcase, clicked it closed, and put it up in the luggage rack. And Julia and Hulda sat close together with Julia's arm through Hulda's, and Julia looked up at Hulda filled with joy, a very special sort of joy.

Here they were together, because somehow Julia had gotten Hulda back on the train again.

(Continued in *That Julia Redfern*)